Best wi[shes]
Roger
Your old Pal

[signature]

March 2016

THE PORCUPINE MAN

Peter Sellers

novum ▲ pro

This book is also available as e-book.

w w w . n o v u m - p u b l i s h i n g . c o . u k

© 2015 novum publishing

ISBN 978-3-99048-351-0
Editor: Arun Natarajan
Cover photo: Jonathan Sellers
Cover design, layout & typesetting: novum publishing

www.novum-publishing.co.uk

CONTENTS

Prologue   7
Chapter 1
   RETREAT TO VALHALLA   9
Chapter 2
   SWALLOWING THE FLY 21
Chapter 3
   DELVING INTO THE MIRE 43
Chapter 4
   THE CODICIL 47
Chapter 5
   THE PROFESSOR'S DILEMMA 61
Chapter 6
   THE SLOUGH OF DESPOND 79
Chapter 7
   JUDGEMENT OF SOLOMON 87
Chapter 8
   CRY HAVOC AND LET SLIP
   THE DOGS OF WAR 95
Chapter 9
   ILLUMINATING THE DARKNESS 99
Chapter 10
   ALL IS LOST SAVE HONOUR 105
Epilogue 109

PROLOGUE

In the midst of the present international turmoil there are a multitude of despotic rulers, fanatical religious leaders and corrupt politicians whose sole aim is to attack and eliminate, by any means at their disposal, all democratic regimes, equitable and fair legal systems, sexual equality and perhaps, far more significantly, all contrary religious views.

Thoroughly evil and completely unscrupulous, their unashamed dogma is to pursue their own narrow ideological interests by forcing their own strict, distorted and regressive religious beliefs on others and at the same time denying any essence of democracy to those under their governance. Their controlling leaders impose their will by ruthlessly inflicting massacres, hostage taking, all types of extreme violence, corruption, kidnapping, fraud and even sexual exploitation with the sole aim of forcing all objectors to wholly accept their beliefs, invariably resulting in the violent disintegration and destruction of the lives of countless innocent men, women and children.

One has only to open the pages of our daily newspapers to be reminded of the horrendous atrocities, inflicted daily, upon innocent men, women and young children by these zealots, operating under the banners of al-Muhajiroun, Boko Haram, Al-Qaeda, Isis and other kindred organisations, often misguidedly financially aided and abetted by certain unscrupulous leaders of the Sunni, Kurd and Shia factions who, by taking advantage of the region's chaos, are themselves inciting mayhem particularly, in and around Lybia, Syria and Iraq.

The immeasurable suffering, caused to religious minorities and to countless millions of homeless refugees, directly or indirectly resulting from the actions of these few manipulative leaders, is increasing day by day.

Their complete disregard for irreplaceable ancient sculptures and other works of art, most of which were configured and erected by their own ancestors, is a clear demonstration of their destructive and negative ethos.

Each and every recorded atrocity clearly demonstrates the continuing impotence of America, Great Britain and many like-minded countries, to even mitigate these problems, never mind produce any viable long term solution.

If the question was ever posed, to even the most peace-loving, gentle and considerate of people they would, however reluctantly, have to admit that the world would be a significantly better, safer and more peaceful planet if these evil and controlling individuals could, somehow, be eliminated from the society in general.

The removal of even a significant number of these zealots and despots would drastically reduce their influence upon their susceptible, misguided followers who sadly include an increasing number of the world's most vulnerable, and impressionable young.

The free world, and perhaps even some less democratic regimes, have their own leaders who would, under pressure, reluctantly admit to be only too willing to condone and even actively support the removal of these dangerous leaders, who are currently and vehemently initiating and then perpetuating mayhem and chaos in these extremely vulnerable areas of the world.

The problem is that those same world leaders would only contemplate sanctioning direct action, such as the assassination of these undesirables, if an absolutely certain and fool-proof method could be found.

For such a method to be remotely acceptable it would have to defy all detection and, far more importantly, ensure that no blame could ever be traced back both to the perpetrator and, more importantly, to all those who had sanctioned such drastic action.

Has this silent and undetectable method of execution already been achieved, albeit by a unique fluke of nature, in the human form of ...
The Porcupine Man?

Chapter 1

RETREAT TO VALHALLA

A humid July day was drawing to its close when George Deakin, his normally genial face displaying unmistakable signs of inner mental strain, drove his ageing blue Volvo automatic slowly upwards towards his remote log cabin retreat, located deep within in the High Peak District of Derbyshire.

The compact split-level log cabin was situated in complete isolation, sheltered deep within the myriad of dark green Scots Pines and the somewhat lighter tinted Japanese Larches which haphazardly cloaked the sloping rocky hillside.

George's cabin occupied what was previously a roughly cleared plot of land at the far end of this long winding, and now somewhat neglected, dirt track.

This narrow, barely adequate access road, leading from the tarmac road to the cabin, had been roughly excavated and stoned many years ago from the virgin land and now featured many pot holes and ruts, the result of the previous hard winter.

The uneven surface rocked and jolted even the well-sprung luxury car, requiring George's careful negotiation of the twists and turns which led upwards to his isolated, but very picturesque, log cabin complete with its attached solidly constructed garage which George had added some years previously using the local limestone.

During its laboured up-hill progress, the delicate overhanging fronds of the drooping branches of the pines and larches, continually brushed against the car's windscreen leaving streaks of rainbow coloured droplets on the already dirty glass, causing it to sparkle intermittently when caught by the dying sun's rays darting through the restless trees.

George's previous efforts to clean his windscreen during his last Motorway stop had been rendered ineffectual by the stubborn ingrained greasy surface, the result of many long hours of hard motorway driving in his desperate escape to his personal Valhalla.

At some appreciable distance from his cabin, George impatiently prodded at the red button of his remote control to initiate the upward motion of the garage's roller-shuttered door.

It was eight months since his last visit so he was quite relieved to see the articulated teak-oiled wooden slats eventually slowly shudder upwards within their greased metal guides, gradually revealing the natural limestone interior.

George Deakin had used this attractive hide-a-way many times over the years to escape from the ever present demands of his scientific work, although less frequently due to him being increasingly required to work for extended periods conducting important scientific, medically orientated projects overseas.

When engaged on these intensive and energy draining scientific commissions for major drug companies he was always comforted by the knowledge that, on his return to the United Kingdom, his little cabin would welcome him within the solitude of its pine logged walls allowing some escape and, for a little time at least, some respite from the demanding pressures of the outside world by enabling George to completely surrender to its restful solitude.

He slowly inched the car through the rather restricted opening, its bodywork now badly streaked with traces of muddy water from the numerous puddles resulting from the recent heavy rains, eventually coming to rest on the uneven, oil splattered stone flagged floor.

Immediately, he had cleared the entrance impatiently, and somewhat thankfully, pressed the same button which now caused the door to roll squeakily down the rusty steel guides, finally coming to rest on the uneven threshold. This involuntary action to immediately lower the door behind him, shrouding him in the gloom of the garage was indicative of his inner anxiety, caused by his present predicament.

George did not make any effort to move from his seat for several minutes, closing his eyes and leaning back he emotionally embraced the protective solid stone construction of the interior of his garage.

The mere act of experiencing the closing door gradually but surely shrouding him in the semi-darkness of the interior made George feel relatively secure for the first time in many months.

During the long car journey from his Cambridge bachelor flat, housed within the secret and obscure scientific complex where he had been working, his mind had been continuously racked and tormented by silently debating the rapidly reducing alternative courses of action that still remained open to him in his current, potentially life threatening, situation.

Mentally brushing aside the personal danger which could result, he had finally understood that he had no other alternative but to warn the public, through contacting those in authority who he believed would listen, about the sinister and unique situation into which he had become personally embroiled.

Even though he realised that he may never be able to return to his beloved country again, he had become absolutely convinced, that running away from his responsibilities without first fully disclosing his story was not an option his conscience could tolerate.

Sliding out of his warm leather seat with a resigned sigh, he closed the door of the Volvo behind him with a resounding thud and walked purposefully to the rear and opened the boot, which held his minimal necessities for his expected minimal stay.

Somewhat hampered by his overnight case, rucksack and brief case, he walked towards the rear breeze-block partition fire-wall, which separated the garage from his living quarters, and fumbled in the semi-darkness to depress the timed light switch which allowed some dim light from the dusty, cobwebbed covered bulkhead fitting to pierce the gloom of the interior.

With some more fumbling, he eventually removed his house key from the brass hook, hidden for added security behind an old picture of his family home.

At the stout wooden fire door, leading to cabin's living quarters; he turned the key, simultaneously depressing the metal handle to enter his cosy lounge.

After carefully wiping his feet on the horse-hair mat, he strode purposefully into the main cabin area, carrying his overnight bag, his canvas rucksack together with his voluminous leather brief case swinging from a leather strap over his shoulder.

Looking around the room, the grimy windows and general dusty appearance of the interior of the main cabin both puzzled and annoyed George in turn, causing him to momentarily make himself a promise to gently chastise Ruth Murray, his elderly, and previously extremely conscientious, cleaning lady.

George paid Ruth through arranged regular direct debits from his bank and had enjoyed the services of this pleasant and conscientious widow for many years. She had visited his lodge weekly to dust, hoover and generally tidy the small rooms and he had always felt more relaxed with the knowledge that Ruth willingly combined her cleaning duties by keeping a general watch over his retreat, particularly during his long absences abroad. Alas, he was not to know that, very sadly, Ruth had died from a sudden heart attack only two months before his arrival in Derbyshire.

Laying his rucksack, bag and briefcase on the thickly carpeted floor he stretched, sighed and wearily slumped into his favourite dark brown leather easy chair, always situated on the right of the ash-filled, smoke-blackened stone fireplace.

A casual glance disclosed the incorrect time registered on the old wooden mantel clock and he made a mental promise to replace its batteries when he had attended to the other, far more pressing duties that lay before him.

As he leaned back, making the old chair creak, he silently thanked his calor gas heating and timer for at least providing some semblance of warmth, no doubt aided by some residual heat from the recent spell of warm weather.

Emitting a cough, due to a lingering minor chest infection, he rose wearily from his chair and mechanically undid the soft leather straps holding the main flap of the rucksack finally untying the neck-cord to release the contents onto his table.

This well-used and somewhat battered rucksack, a survivor from his many trips abroad, always contained what George called his survival kit for any emergencies, comprising amongst other necessities of life, a battery powered wet-razor, his somewhat mangled tooth brush, some cooling aftershave, shaving gel, hair brush and comb with a small hand towel completing his basic toiletries.

George knew from experience that there would be minimal supplies in the cabin's small refrigerator and an even more limited selection of mundane, unappetising tinned food stacked on the shelves of his old pine kitchen cupboard.

He took a thankful swig from a previously opened three-quarter full bottle of Bells whiskey, again coughing, but this time due to the effect of the pale yellow liquid on his parched throat.

George slowly changed into his comfortable, dark blue towelling robe, which had been hanging inside the bathroom door and reached up to pull on the swinging cord to initiate his electric blow heater. He stared at his reflection in the mirror, noticing his unusually haggard strained features, tired eyes, surmounted by his grey streaked black hair and eventually, after methodically applying some blue shaving gel, slowly and deliberately began to remove the effects of his two day's stubble.

Having carefully dialled his desired water temperature his body was massaged by welcoming needles of warm stimulating jets from his power shower, recently installed at great expense in his luxurious black and white tiled wet room.

George completed his leisurely ablutions and regarded his tanned, now clean shaven face, in the bathroom mirror with far more satisfaction, finally brushing his slightly receding hair line into some semblance of order.

Satisfied, that he had recovered, at least to some degree, his usual poise and confidence which might enable him to more confidently face the daunting, but now absolutely vital task that lay ahead, he towelled his hair dry.

Having his chipped Victorian cast iron bath, purchased on a foolish whim some years ago from the Newark Antique Fair, replaced by this far more convenient method of showering, contained within a more easily managed wet room, was a decision he had never regretted.

Finally, locating a couple of luxurious white Turkish towels from the slotted shelf above the warm cistern cupboard, he slowly and deliberately thoroughly dried himself whilst simultaneously attempting to regroup his scattered thoughts and re-evaluating his current predicament.

With his hands still visibly trembling from the result of the intense mental strain, which had increased to approaching breaking point over the past few days, he paused momentarily with his hand on the brass door handle, before entering his dining cum lounge area, still musing upon what would be his most effectual course of action.

In the situation in which he now found himself George had the great consolation of knowing that he had been extremely careful, even to the point of obsession, in preserving his little cabin's privacy, even from his small circle of friends and acquaintances.

His scientific work, which regularly took him all over the world, was not conducive to cultivating deep and lasting friendships and consequently his amorous relationships were by necessity, and certainly not by choice, spasmodic and rather transient.

But now, in his present perilous situation, his deliberate decision to protect his secret lair from friends and others in the outside world had now been rewarded in spades. That wise decision now afforded him both valuable thinking time, protection and, more importantly, some mental respite during this critical and most dangerous period of his forty-six years of life.

Languishing in his chair, and still experiencing the therapeutic effects of his shower and shave, George felt more relaxed than he had been for many months, fortified and fully prepared to face what could be postponed no longer.

Inevitably, following his long and arduous drive following a restless night at his flat in Cambridge nature could not be denied and, enveloped in the cabin's warmth, his fatigue eventually took over, his eyelids became heavy and drooped, his loosening fingers caused the heavy crystal whisky glass complete with its residue of golden liquid, to gradually slide onto the thickly piled rug allowing George to finally succumb to a few hours of troubled and turbulent sleep.

George awoke suddenly with a shiver, his body obviously sensing the coldness enveloping the room, the result of the ending of the timed heating period of his central heating, and his senses were immediately enlivened by the realisation that he could not delay the inevitable for one second longer.

When he had dressed in a pair of his favourite well-worn jeans and a pale blue fisherman's sweater, purchased from Whitby whilst enjoying a romantic holiday with a dark haired girl named Suzanne, he completed his ensemble by slipping his bare feet into his luxurious pale brown lambs-wool slippers and shuffled from his bedroom into the main living area of his cabin.

He removed his faithful and well used Sony recording machine out of the left hand drawer of one of the matching pair of pine corner cupboards and slowly and deliberately unwound the black cable, finally snapping the plug into one of the spare sockets, situated under his once elegant, but now rather shabby side table.

He plonked himself in the carver chair at the head of his dining table, the high backed unyielding rush seated chair being made a great deal more comfortable by his treasured hand-embroidered cushion, given to him by his dear widowed mother as a Christmas present, some five years back and just prior to her sudden and premature death.

With the back of his sleeve George wiped some gathering beads of perspiration from his brow, the result of the combined effect of his hot shower and some nervous apprehension at the realisation of the onerous task that lay ahead.

After carefully inserting one of the long-playing recording cassettes into the machine George Deakin slowly and deliberately leaned towards the small microphone that was tilted up towards him on the table and began …

… this message is directed to a few specially chosen persons of influence who, whilst being fervent nationalists, I am aware are also avid supporters of the maintenance of high standards of morality in both private and public life.

May I first introduce myself at the same time suggesting that should any further credentials be required these can be easily verified by referring to the internet and searching under my full name, where details of my career to date should add credibility to my words and by doing so validate this urgent message.

I am Dr. George Manjon Deakin FRS D.Sc M.Sc. (Cantab.) lately attached to The Government Special Biological and Scientific Unit SSP 34, Cambridge which, until his death some months ago, operated under the direction of Professor Raymond Quigley where I operated as his deputy, within this same Cambridge Complex.

Under the Professor's ultimate direction I was part of a team engaged on special top secret scientific assignments reporting directly to the Home Office.

I am sending this recording to you as one of ten recipients, all chosen by me, as well-respected leaders of organisations dedicated to the maintenance and furtherance of moral and ethical standards, particularly within the United Kingdom.

It is my sincere, fervent and desperate hope that in sending this recorded information to more than one recipient then surely at least one will not dismiss its contents as the ramblings of some unbalanced mischief maker or deranged "whistle blower".

Should you still retain any doubt concerning the validity of the warnings contained within these recordings may I implore you to immediately make your own detailed, guarded and confidential enquiries into the facts and circumstances contained within this message?

I reiterate that should you make any enquiries I implore you, for your own and your family's safety, to act cautiously and prudently, a warning which will surely be validated as you progress through this recording.

I am fully aware that the story that I am about to relate will seem incredible and possibly, at first hearing, unbelievable ... indeed, I myself, can scarcely comprehend what I have experienced and witnessed with my own eyes, during the past one year or more.

If any further supporting evidence be required to induce your urgent action it could well be the fact that, within the next few days, weeks or months my own death may well be reported, most likely within some obscure press feature and possibly following some bizarre or unforeseen accident.

I gain some small comfort from knowing that, should there be any publicity surrounding my death, as self-prophesied within this recording, this may hopefully serve to provide you and the other recipients with the necessary impetus for just one person to take action without any further delay?

My personal involvement commenced around eighteen months ago when I was recruited as Senior Biological Research Officer, reporting directly to the now late Professor Raymond Quigley and I commenced working within a specially formed highly secret scientific government department near Cambridge.

At the time of my appointment I was informed that my role was to act as Deputy to Professor Quigley, the world-renowned biological scientist and double Nobel Prize winner, engaged on a unique and vital project that had the support from the highest echelons of government.

What I soon discovered, and what is not generally known even within his staff at Cambridge, was that Professor Quigley combined his role within the complex by also acting as the Government's Independent Advisor on germ and biological warfare.

It also became evident, during the course of my working so closely with the Professor, that he had the facility to report directly to the Home Secretary, through a specially designated and secure private telephone line.

Both the Professor and I have both lived through these last few months vainly attempting to manage a situation that has been rapidly spiralling out of our control.

Initially, I must now reluctantly admit, we were both fascinated and intrigued by the scenario we had both helped to create before the stark realisation finally dawned that we had become the mere tools of a system with one concerted aim, which you may find hard to believe without the detailed proof within this recording which was simply ...

... to discover some fool-proof method of controlling a unique biological destructive power contained within a human being and then to proceed from controlling to directing that individual to infect and kill other specifically chosen human beings.

Some months ago you may recollect that the same Professor Quigley, regularly lauded in the press and news items as a brilliant and internationally known scientist, was reported to have tragically perished in a fire at his London home?

The little church, in the Professor's home village of Prestbury, Cheshire, was crammed with colleagues, friends and other eminent scientists from around the world ... Ministers of the Crown were present at his funeral and a junior Minister was even given the honour of presenting the effusive and touching eulogy at his Service.

The previously held Coroner's inquest presented the verdict to the world that the Professor's death was the direct result of an accidental explosion and fire that had occurred as he was presumably conducting some experiment in his laboratory present within the basement of his London home.

The verdict was confirmed by a Senior Officer of the Health and Safety Executive within his written submission to the Coroner and underwritten by a Colonel Thorpe, acting with the authority of the Home Office.

I know, for absolute certainty, that Professor Quigley had died at least four days prior to the reported "accidental" fire at his home and moreover his death was definitely not the result of any accident within his laboratory or even in London.

It is also a fact that, a mere five minutes following the reporting of the explosion and fire by neighbours, his detached home was sealed off from even the police and fire service by the instruction of this, previously mentioned, Colonel Thorpe, acting under the direct authority of the Home Office.

The security and other restrictions immediately imposed at the site were said to be due to the existence of potentially explosive chemicals stored in the Professor's laboratory within the house cellars. Even the Health and Safety Executive, after many abortive protests, was firmly denied access until many days had elapsed and, even then, only when Home Office scientists had completed their own lengthy and meticulous investigations and many items had been removed from the site.

All these preliminary forensic investigations were carried out under the personal direction of this shadowy figure, Colonel Thorpe ... a person who will continue to be mentioned throughout my continuing story.

It is worth mentioning that at the inquest, all the Professor's neighbours who had heard the explosions and witnessed the resulting fire, all stressed that the fire had burned with an incredible ferocity, far beyond what they would have expected from a normal house fire, and the whole detached property had been reduced to a smouldering and blackened shell.

Even the local fire station Chief Officer, when closely questioned by the coroner to explain why no fire fighters had immediately attended the fire, vaguely explained that it was at the direct instructions of a Colonel Thorpe who was present at the scene. The officer added that these instructions were supported by official documentation confirming that the Colonel was acting with the full authority of The Home Office.

This officer was a somewhat evasive and unconvincing witness, possibly embarrassed by the almost universal criticism of his force's lack of action on the night.

Following a short adjournment, during which the officer was seen in deep conversation with Colonel Thorpe, he returned to the stand and explained his force's non-action by the fact that he had been given prior warning that there could have been some explosive mixtures stored within the Professor's laboratory and any attempt to approach the building to extinguish the blaze would have placed his officers in a situation involving unacceptable and unquantifiable risks.

He confirmed to the Coroner in answer to his question, that in not allowing his men to even dampen down the fire the next day, he was acting at all times under the strict instructions of the same Colonel Thorpe.

A most bizarre incident occurred towards the end of the Hearing, when the coroner requested Colonel Thorpe to take the stand to answer some further vital questions.

The coroner was handed a letter by his clerk and, following a short adjournment, the coroner stated that Colonel Thorpe had presented detailed written evidence which rendered a personal statement in court unnecessary and which now allowed him to record an official verdict of accidental death due to a house fire.

To this day I am sure that the whole charade, including the fire, was a concerted and well-organised effort by the authorities, possibly the Home Office, under the direct control of the aforementioned Colonel Thorpe, to dispose of an already dead Professor Quigley.

Moreover, I am absolutely convinced that the body of the Professor was brought to his London home from the area where he had died, days previously, and then placed within the laboratory, prior to the explosion and fire.

I am also practically certain that the house fire was started intentionally by a person or persons unknown, but acting under the direct instructions of Colonel Thorpe with the aim of destroying a deadly infection that was still active within the Professor's dead body.

Chapter 2

SWALLOWING THE FLY

I have no need to remind my listeners that we are all aware that the world is experiencing volatile and dangerous times.

Commencing with the New York, Twin-Towers disaster, there has been further turmoil in Afghanistan, Iraq, Aden and Syria involving Boko Haram, Isis and similar movements and organisations, not least the previous attacks on the United Kingdom by the al-Muhajiroun organisation.

Consequently, the pressure on our own and allied governments to control and if possible incapacitate these organisations by removing their leaders has increased dramatically.

These movements have already killed, and are continuing to kill the innocent, making whole populations homeless as well as incurring the West and their Allies in enormous costs, both materially and financially.

It is accepted that all democratic countries together with many neighbouring countries and regimes, that are threatened by these organisations and rogue states, controlled by their ruthless and extremist leaders, would clutch at any possible solution that could lead to the elimination of these rogue leaders without the need to invade and become embroiled in unpopular extended campaigns, as exemplified by the disastrous Iraq and Afghanistan wars.

Invasions to fight and defeat these sects, by employing troops on the ground, are still politically abhorrent, in view of the hard lessons still being learned, not least through the catastrophic state of affairs that has emerged following the Iraq debacle and to a lesser extent, Syria and Afghanistan.

Uprisings by militants, each with their own agenda, have exacerbated the spread of chaos and mayhem throughout many neighbouring regions which were previously peaceful, thriving and reasonably tolerant to other religions.

The consequence is that an urgent solution to defeat these rogue organisations had to be urgently found, and the Professor and I unwittingly became embroiled in providing the solution which was then adopted by a lunatic faction within the establishment, headed by this aforementioned Colonel Thorpe which, if actually implemented, could have disastrous and unforeseeable consequences.

George Deakin paused in order to adjust the position of the microphone, at the same time wiping some slight perspiration from his brow and take a deep gulp from his now warm mineral water as he continued his narrative ...

... It was just over a year ago, following a short but very intriguing introductory telephone call requesting a meeting, that I received a caller at my London flat ... a lone man standing upon my door step turned out to be the aforementioned Colonel Thorpe.

Even at our very first encounter Colonel Thorpe exuded a disturbing and sinister presence ... heightened by his thin sallow face and piercing eyes surmounted by sleeked back, black hair.

After I had taken charge of his Burberry rain coat and fringed long silk scarf, embellished by a series of small red shields presumably denoting some University College, my visitor sat down in the nearest easy chair.

Without even asking my permission to smoke, The Colonel carefully placed a black cheroot in a short silver-ended amber holder, finally igniting the cheroot with a flourish using a somewhat ostentatious and expensive gold DuPont lighter.

His well-cut fawn jacket, with gold-linked white shirt cuffs protruding slightly from the sleeves, spoke with an elegant good taste that only a bespoke tailor could produce and, together with the well pressed and elegantly cut slacks, polished black elastic sided shoes he presented himself as a well-dressed, rather vain, man of the establishment.

Pocketing his lighter, leaning back into his chair and drawing deeply on the glowing cheroot, Thorpe then explained that he had heard, on the scientific grape vine that my current overseas research contract was nearing completion and that I might be seeking a further challenging position within the pharmaceutical industry.

A Government department was urgently seeking a man with my qualifications and experience to join a vitally important research team which was currently engaged on top secret and ground-breaking work, aligned to my own specialist area concerning tropical diseases.

He explained further that there was already a small hand-picked research team operating under the direction of a Professor Raymond Quigley.

Thorpe remarked that he was certain that, due to my being engaged in similar work, I would be fully aware of the Professor's reputation.

Professor Quigley now very urgently required a colleague, with my own particular specialised knowledge and expertise, to act in the very important role of his Deputy and Personal Assistant.

Immediately, this Colonel Thorpe had my unswerving attention ... the very mention of the name Professor Raymond Quigley was, as most if not all of my listeners must surely be aware, is synonymous with the most highly regarded and renowned scientist in the field of tropical and associated diseases, having already been recognised by being honoured by the award of two Nobel Prizes for his service to science.

Throughout the course of our meeting the Colonel was extremely secretive and non-committal, to the point of annoyance, emphasising that whilst I was the Professor's first choice for the position, due to its very sensitive nature all details would need to be discussed on a person to person basis with the man himself.

I must readily admit that my ego was flattered beyond belief to believe that Professor Quigley had even heard of my work and moreover, that such an eminent scientist wished to discuss my working so closely with him on what appeared, based on the very minimal information so far released by the Colonel, to be a very significant project.

Vainly trying to disguise my enthusiasm I readily agreed with Colonel Thorpe that he should contact the Professor without further delay to arrange a convenient time and place for the Professor and me to fully discuss the precise nature of the project and, more importantly, what was to be my own particular role.

The venue, proposed by Professor Quigley and immediately accepted by me, was the Colonnade Hotel, a quiet but luxurious hotel in Maida Vale, situated within the area of London's Little Venice.

I was quite familiar with this hostelry, having regularly stayed at the Colonnade, during my visits to the capital.

In fact, during one of my stays, I had some interesting discussions with the Manager and my long time historical interest was stirred by his disclosure, that when the Colonnade Hotel was originally a nursing home, it was the birth place of the Bletchley Park genius Alan Turing, instrumental in the cracking of the Enigma Code during the Second World War.

This fascinating information certainly explained the unusual dimensions of the hotel lift, designed to accommodate the hospital's long wheeled stretchers during their passage to and from the various floors.

Coincidentally, I later discovered that the Professor had also stayed at the Colonnade once or twice to meet with fellow scientists visiting London, which probably explained why he had mentioned the hotel as one of his alternative venues?

True to his word, I received an email from Colonel Thorpe the next day to confirm that he had booked two single rooms, in the names of the Professor and myself, for the following Friday night to enable us to discuss all relevant matters regarding the potential post at Cambridge, in a convivial and relaxed atmosphere.

On the appointed evening, around 6.30 pm, I paid off my taxi and walked into the Colonnade's well lit and welcoming reception area and asked for the Professor by name at the desk and was duly directed towards a table at the far corner of the lounge, where the venerable Professor was already seated, complete with an opened bottle of Chardonnay languishing within an ice bucket.

One glass had already been filled from which he had taken a few sips and seeing me approach he poured some of the wine into the remaining glass.

Shaking my hand and beaming a welcome he beckoned the porter to take my coat and bags to the deluxe single room previously reserved for me for that night.

I was somewhat relieved to find that Raymond Quigley who, with his well-worn Harris Tweed suit and brown well-polished brogues, projected the bearing of a country gentleman, was also endowed with a pleasant and unassuming manner, which I warmed to immediately. It soon became obvious that his easy-going veneer concealed a very sharp and perceptive intellect and that he was making a special effort to put me at my ease.

Momentarily, excusing himself, the Professor walked over to the hotel Manager, who was leaning over the reception desk arranging some files, and engaged him in a private conversation whilst I gently stroked the purring hotel cat, which had made its presence known by continually brushing against my trouser legs … a cat, well known to patrons as the venerable and aptly named Mouse.

Continuing to stroke the soft warm marmalade fur I sipped my chilled wine with mounting excitement coupled with some apprehension in anticipation of the next stage of the Professor's interview as well as hopefully being furnished with all the missing details about what my position at Cambridge would entail.

After some further pleasantries we drifted downstairs to partake of our dinner in the intimately lit dining room. The table was tastefully prepared, with a small reserved sign in hand written script propped up against a central bowl of fresh flowers. After ordering our meal we awaited its delivery with some generalised small talk which allowed both of us to gain a general overview of our lives, hobbies and professional interests.

I remember little of our meal, due to my understandable apprehension, coupled with my natural inquisitiveness and anticipation concerning my proposed position, particularly as it involved working in such close co-operation with such a truly eminent scientist.

The Professor quickly reviewed his past work for the government in very general terms but, somewhat to my growing irritation, completely lacking in the required detail for me to properly consider what precise role I was expected to fill, should I decide to accept the post.

In hindsight, it should have been obvious, given that we were in a public dining area, it would not have been prudent for the Professor to disclose the personal and confidential details required for my consideration. It was only when we had finally retired to the privacy of his hotel room and comfortably seated and soothed with an excellent brandy that finally the Professor, slowly and methodically, began to put the flesh on the bones of the elements of the secret and specialised work in which he wanted me to participate.

He disclosed that, for many years, he had been in charge of significant high level and ground-breaking scientific research for the government, involving a disturbing and growing number of rare tropical diseases, many of which still appeared to be immune to all known antidotes and vaccines.

Explaining that, some weeks ago he had been specially directed by Colonel Thorpe, with the tacit support of certain very influential government ministers, to remove himself from all current research and devote all his time and effort in the direction of just one new patient, who had recently been placed in the complex's intensive care ward.

He continued his narrative by explaining that the patient in question was extremely ill from life threatening complications, following a self-poisoning suicide attempt.

Due to him having to devote his whole attention towards this newly admitted high-priority patient and, at the same time having all his senior personnel fully occupied in attending to six other patients within other areas of the complex, it was becoming impossible for him to cope without a Deputy.

He reiterated that the situation was becoming desperate and, even though I was his preferred choice, I perhaps could now appreciate why he needed my positive decision that very evening.

I was somewhat bemused when he disclosed that his interest in me was entirely due to having read, within several important and influential scientific journals, most of my research papers detailing rare and obscure tropical diseases that I had encountered during my scientific commissions in Asia, China and South America.

I cannot deny that I was extremely flattered by his disclosure that he had both read and apparently was actually impressed by their content. But, even then, I still failed to see how my extremely specialised research and expertise could possibly assist in the treatment of this particular patient, however important he seemed to appear.

He clarified the position when he emphasised that I would require far more detailed information of his patient's symptoms and medical history but, as the majority of the information was classified as top secret, I would have to take a great deal at face value, giving his personal assurance that the post being offered was significant and worthy of my obvious talents.

Should I agree to accept the post that night then, and only then, would I be allowed full and unrestrained access to all the files and medical history relevant to this particular patient.

He was adamant that, having read my articles recording my experiences, gained over my many years of operations within the African and Brazilian jungles in dealing with pernicious infections, my expert knowledge would be of great advantage in arriving at a consensus about the most effective course of treatment for his patient.

Quigley greatly surprised me by demonstrating his depth of knowledge of the work I had undertaken involving many obscure and rare diseases whilst working for several pharmaceutical companies all of which, he assured me, had commended my work.

He recognised that these companies were obviously more motivated by potential commercial rewards rather than altruistic reasons but this did not lessen, in any way, the validity of the conclusions expressed within my articles.

At the time I must admit to being somewhat uneasy and even slightly annoyed at the scope and depth of the Professor's information and knowledge about my working life. It was not the information he disclosed involving my professional life that caused me concern but rather his awareness regarding my private life that touched a raw nerve.

It was obvious that the Professor had been extremely well briefed, presumably by the mysterious Colonel Thorpe and his minions, disturbingly proving to me that they must have had me under extremely close surveillance for some considerable time.

However, any lingering doubts or concerns that these disclosures had engendered were eventually quelled, helped by the effects of the second bottle of the excellent Chardonnay and some appeasing comments from the apologetic Professor who must have recognised some growing vexation in my demeanour.

He explained, at some length, that as the position being offered was extremely important and highly sensitive it required a candidate, not only with proven expertise in my specialised field of research, but also possessing impeccable personal credentials.

The Professor emphasised my current bachelor status, adding that it was advantageous to all concerned that I had minimal personal ties or family responsibilities, due to the fact that the work I was being asked to sign up to would most certainly entail long and unsocial hours within a very restricted and controlled environment.

He was sure that I must readily appreciate that the secrecy of the research, combined with the unpredictable hours would inevitably have placed a great strain on any existing close relationship.

Even the Professor's absolute insistence that, should I decide to accept the position that night, I would be required to move immediately from my comfortable flat in London's West Hampstead to the facility in Cambridgeshire, did little to diminish my growing excitement and enthusiasm for the post.

The Contract of Engagement Professor Quigley handed over for my perusal contained very generous terms including, I noticed, a substantial completion bonus together with two stapled added pages of special clauses, incorporating the conditions of the Official Secrets Act in small print.

As I neither had the time, nor the inclination, to peruse all these terms and conditions I merely glanced at the two added pages without realising their true import, apart from noticing that the length of the contract period appeared to be "open-ended" and, perhaps foolishly, took the Professor on trust.

Appreciating by this time that he had "caught his fish" Quigley dismissed my few remaining minor protestations with a wave of his hand reiterating that, such was the need for absolute security, they required the immediate severing of all day to day contact with all my friends and relatives until the conclusion of my contract.

He added that my contract period of employment would be wholly dependent upon the health and progress of our mystery patient which was bizarrely emphasised by Professor Quigley to be the sole reason for my engagement.

Quigley suggested that it would be preferable for me to immediately inform all my close relatives and friends that I would shortly be embarking on a minimum six-month overseas trip to undertake some research for an unnamed commercial company and, due to the remoteness of my destination, I would be unable to be contacted or make contact until my return to the UK.

Finally, both our signatures were appended and duly witnessed by the summoned hotel Manager and his secretary.

The formalities completed, the meeting was brought to a conclusion by Professor Quigley handing me a wallet containing several colour photographs of the laboratories, hospital wards and other facilities, seemingly all contained within the extensive, ivy-clad stone walled grounds of the Ministry's Private Experimental Laboratories in the vicinity of Cambridge. I was somewhat taken aback when I was informed, in response to my natural query, that the facility had no postal address.

Now that I was on board the Professor enlightened me concerning funding for our particular research by explaining that no limit had been imposed on costs, a far cry from my previous experiences within the private sector by having to continuously fight for funding.

I must say that these positive points concerning my engagement blunted all my potential objections to his absolute insistence that I should not even return to my London flat the next day as arrangements had already been made for us both to proceed directly to Cambridgeshire to commence our work.

Sensing my hesitation, the Professor added that this should surely present no problem due to the fact that I was single with no current girlfriend, had no dependencies and moreover my employer had already previously been approached, in anticipation of this meeting, and they had been persuaded that the nation's need had a prior call upon my services.

Quigley informed me that the Ministry would either purchase my flat, at above the market price, or arrange a rewarding rental arrangement through their own agency, adding that he now only required the key to my flat, together with any installed alarm code, in order that arrangements could be immediately put in hand.

I was readily assured that all my files and belongings, would be carefully boxed, secured, collected and deposited within my spacious new four roomed flat within the grounds of the complex.

When we were finally alone in the Professor's suite, both of us feeling a great deal more relaxed now that all the details involving my new position had been finalised, the Professor poured out two glasses of vintage port and drank to my health, adding with a grin that he hoped our personal and professional relationship would be as agreeable and fruitful as the port.

After some further general chatting the Professor suggested that it had been a long and tiring day for us both and that we would benefit from a good night's sleep in preparation for our journey to Cambridge the following morning.

Wishing each other goodnight we retired to our rooms.

Elated by the anticipation of my new and intriguing appointment and with my ablutions completed I thankfully enveloped myself in the soft duvet, suddenly tired and mentally drained and yet conscious that there remained a myriad of questions that I had failed to ask and consequently remained unanswered.

Following a restless night, I would have been loath to leave my warm covers had I not been fully aware that Quigley would be expecting my arrival at breakfast in preparation for an agreed early start. I reluctantly dragged on my dressing gown and opened the thick heavy bedroom curtains to disclose a bright morning with little breeze, suggesting another warm dry day ahead.

As I shaved and showered, notwithstanding all the assurances I had been given the previous evening, I now admit to some unaccountable and lingering apprehension about what the future held ... this concern was soon to intensify and eventually horrifically be justified over the succeeding months!

When I eventually arrived, a little late, at the breakfast area Professor Quigley was already seated at a corner table, complete with fruit juice and scanning the Daily Telegraph, frowning at the stark headlines which disclosed the continuing unsettled state of the world.

His face quickly broke into a smile when he saw me approach signalling me to make my choice of breakfast, adding with a wink that, as I was now dining at the Government's expense, I could afford the full breakfast.

We enjoyed a leisurely meal whilst engaging in small talk and, after a quick glance at his gold Omega Sea Master de Ville, which I had admired the previous evening, he suggested that we each retired to our rooms to complete our packing to allow for our departure to Cambridge in around half-an-hour.

Once we had arrived in the reception area Professor Quigley settled both our accounts with his Gold Visa debit card, thanked the young lady receptionist and pointed out our luggage to a heavily built, grey haired man, who had been seated quietly in a corner seat in reception, later to be introduced to me as Harold.

Harold who, in the absence of any other information, I assumed to be our official driver from Cambridge, was dressed in a somewhat crumpled but functional well-cut dark suit surmounted by a black shiny peaked cap, devoid of any identifying insignia.

After completing some cursory introductions the Professor and I seated ourselves comfortably in the back of a black Range Rover and, with only a slight nod to the Professor, the taciturn Harold carefully closed our door and on his way round to the driver's seat slammed closed the fully loaded boot. Our chauffeur, after donning a pair of ancient sunglasses, slid behind the wheel and we were soon leaving London and the Colonnade Hotel far behind, gliding off towards the M11 and our destination.

I could not help but notice our driver, Harold, was completely cut off from any rear-seat conversation by a thick pale green glass screen, which appeared to be replicated in all of the car's rear windows.

The Professor used an intercom, presumably the sole means of communicating with Harold, to give some further instruction regarding our expected time of our arrival at the laboratory complex and then, giving me a reassuring smile, sat back in the yielding black leather seat.

When we were well on our way, following a long period of reflective silence, Professor Quigley began to explain, in more detail, about the work he was engaged upon and the role that I was expected to perform, but in a generalised way and still lacking the fine detail that I impatiently awaited.

After we had driven for just over an hour we turned into a short narrow drive leading from the minor country road and soon approached a pair of huge and very elaborate ornamental gilded wrought iron gates set in heavy metal jambs within a high stone wall.

The wall was further surmounted by a patterned wrought iron railing with some undisguised evidence of electrified protection.

Our car slowed and stopped at the first of two security boxes immediately in front of the gates, which were occupied by uniformed personnel to whom Harold handed over a black leather wallet, presumably containing some identification, and it was only after the Professor had entered a security code into a blue box that was handed to him through the car window, that we were allowed to continue on our way.

As we commenced our journey up the drive I noticed, in the rear view mirror, that one of the guards was engaged in a telephone conversation which I presumed was to advise someone that our arrival was imminent.

During our journey from the gatehouse I could not fail to be aware of the intermittent blinking of security camera lenses dotted at intervals along the whole length of the driveway.

We travelled slowly for about half a mile up this tarmac road which was lined on each side with alternately spaced mature oak and beech trees, all with a backdrop of spacious lawns being relentlessly manicured by grazing sheep.

Eventually we were deposited, along with our luggage, in front of a metal studded door, situated within a quadrangle, which I soon discovered was the main entrance to a series of flats, all sympathetically converted within a 17th century stable block. After a short conversation concerning our next meeting, the Professor detailed yet another security man to attend to his own luggage, whilst Harold assisted me with my cases into my designated flat, resisting all my efforts to engage in any small talk.

I spent the rest of the day settling in and organising the minimal toiletries and clothing I had brought from the hotel, hoping that my other personal belongings would not take too long in arriving from my flat in London.

I then watched some television whilst eating a quite reasonable meal, that Harold had left with me contained within a small pannier, washed down with a small bottle of wine from my well-stocked mini bar.

Having showered I found the bed inviting and enjoyed an early and restful night.

The following day I felt much more at home when all my personal items had been duly delivered from my London flat, all efficiently sealed within wooden boxes, marked fragile, exactly as the Professor had promised during our meeting at the Colonnade Hotel.

I was both gratified and extremely impressed with the efficiency deployed as evidenced by the fact that all of my possessions had been so promptly recovered and all appeared to have been packed securely and efficiently.

With my worldly goods safely ensconced I finally began to feel at home in my new surroundings, the only slightly disconcerting feature of my new abode was the sight of heavy wrought iron grills at each and every window of my flat, apparent when I drew back the thick blue velvet curtains on my first morning.

Although my first working day with the Professor was scheduled to commence at 10.30 am, thoughtfully allowing me time to unpack my delivered boxes, I had no idea where I had to go and was somewhat relieved when a chauffeur driven car arrived at my flat at 10.15 am and deposited me at the laboratory's main entrance.

Even though I had not yet been supplied with any identifying documents I was obviously expected and one of the security guards ushered me into the Professor's large and well-appointed inner sanctum.

With a beaming smile Professor Quigley welcomed me and after handing me an official pass and other necessary identification papers, all contained in an impressive leather wallet, he gradually began to fill in some of the missing details of what was expected of me in my dual role of his Deputy and Chief Assistant.

It is ingrained in my mind, and will remain so for the remainder of my life, that it was on this momentous day that the Professor mentioned, for the very first time, the name of our special patient, a Leonard Selby, who apparently was the sole reason for my urgent recruitment and my presence in Cambridge.

To say, I was completely flabbergasted by his belated disclosure that all this fuss was due to a single middle aged suicidal patient, is an understatement and my bafflement must have been apparent to the Professor.

At that time it seemed completely unbelievable that all this security, at enormous cost to the tax payer, was due to the illness, however exceptional, of one seemingly insignificant middle-aged man.

Noticing the intense disappointment etched on my face Professor Quigley, placed both hands on my shoulders and looked me straight in the eyes saying that he fully understood my dilemma and asked for my continuing patience.

He then proceeded, slowly and methodically, to fill in the missing elements of the case which initially intrigued me and finally succeeding in igniting my significant medical interest in our very special patient.

Leonard Selby, it was explained, had been brought to his attention some four months ago as a result of an old friend and ex-colleague, Brian Price, a Consultant Oncologist within a London teaching hospital.

Price, a highly regarded middle-aged consummate professional, had telephoned him to say that he had recently become involved with a unique and puzzling case of self-inflicted poisoning which was not really his field of expertise.

His reason for contacting Professor Quigley was due to the bizarre situation that had developed subsequent to Selby becoming his patient and Price had requested they should meet urgently to discuss his patient's latest symptoms and hopefully obtain some advice concerning possible further treatment.

Price explained that Leonard Selby's condition, following several days in intensive care, had developed to a stage that was both unique and somewhat alarming.

Selby appeared to be suffering from a catastrophic whole-body infection, initially categorised as some type of advanced septicaemia or sepsis that defied medical explanation. The infection began to develop into a condition that Price, with all his experience and knowledge of tumours, had never previously encountered.

Price had repeated during their telephone conversation that he required some urgent advice and with Quigley's professional interest now thoroughly aroused, the Professor had suggested that the meeting should be held the next day, when he was already programmed to be in London.

The meeting was held at Price's consulting rooms in the early afternoon which were conveniently situated near the London Clinic where the Professor had been presenting a pre-arranged morning lecture on Ebola and other related diseases.

During the afternoon he had listened intently to Price's story, which was at times extremely sad but simultaneously, to a medical professional, intriguing.

Price then handed Professor Quigley a copy of the copious notes he had taken on the whole history of the Leonard Selby case, including carefully indexed interviews with neighbours, paramedics, police officers and nursing staff involved with this strange and unique case.

The Professor had listened to his colleague's long exposition without interruption with the concentration and patience of one used to hearing similar case notes in his own consulting rooms.

Price commenced by explaining that Leonard Selby, a qualified chemist of around 58 years old, was the owner of a small but reasonably profitable chain of Chemist Shops situated around shopping centres within the area of West London.

Of somewhat ordinary appearance and demeanour, Selby had lived with his wife Norma enjoying a comfortable, if somewhat predictable and mundane existences, within the bustling area of Cricklewood, near the exit of the M1 motorway.

The couple doted on their only child, Frank Charles Selby, an Oxford Graduate with a 1st Class Honours Degree which had rewarded him by being offered a well-paid position with Bear Sterns in the United States, a firm who advised companies and wealthy investors regarding potentially rewarding investments in ground breaking biochemical projects.

The Selby's whole life revolved round their son and they took pride in regularly being updated about Frank's work and his many accomplishments.

But their lives had been suddenly turned into turmoil when they received devastating official confirmation that their son Frank had been amongst the 130 victims of a plane crash in an area between Syria and Jordan, carried out, and brazenly admitted, by an Islamic terrorist organisation.

Tragedy followed on tragedy for poor Leonard when his wife Norma, already in fragile health, died suddenly the following week in the local hospital following a severe stroke.

Leonard was inconsolable, being absolutely convinced that his wife's death had been due to the shock and distress of learning about the circumstances surrounding the death of their one and only child.

Leonard Selby, quite understandably, became increasingly depressed, finding little to live for now that the two people nearest to his heart had died in quick succession, and in such sudden and tragic circumstances.

Continuing his story Price had related that over the ensuing months Leonard Selby had apparently become reclusive and increasingly neglectful to his business, personal needs and comforts which obviously had caused growing concern to his family doctor, friends and neighbours.

Finally, after spurning some suggested psychological counselling and other medical help, his depression eventually must have led him to decide to end his life by taking doses of multiple poisons, all readily available to him from his own Chemist shops.

Hearing a commotion, coupled with an horrific scream during the early hours of the morning, his concerned neighbours had called both the police and ambulance services, and when eventually the front door was forced open, poor Selby was found lying semi-conscious in the entrance hall surrounded by ample evidence of, what later was to be established by the Coroner, his chosen method of suicide ... numerous half empty poison bottles scattered around his deeply unconscious body.

Even though the attending paramedics were convinced, due to the quantity and variety of substances he would have consumed, that Selby's condition was terminal, due to the fact that there were some slight indications of life, Leonard Selby was rushed to the nearest hospital, where Price held the post of a Senior Consultant.

Price further informed the Professor that it was later ascertained by the local forensic laboratory, during their preparation for the anticipated Coroner's inquest that, from the evidence of the recovered opened bottles and packages scattered around Selby, a cocktail of perhaps some twenty or even thirty noxious fluids could quite possibly have been consumed by Leonard Selby.

By extreme good fortune, Brian Price said he happened to be on duty at the hospital that early morning and he had immediately placed Leonard Selby into the high dependency section of the intensive care ward.

Even though absolutely convinced that it was only a matter of time, Price was aware that he should at least attempt some basic treatment in an effort to make Leonard Selby as comfortable as possible. The treatment he prescribed included stomach pumping and the injection of certain speculative antidotes, in order to comply with both his duty of care to his patient and his medical responsibilities to the hospital.

He reiterated to Professor Quigley that, whilst his patient had been immediately rushed to the high dependency ward section and a team of four had deployed every possible effort made to resuscitate him, they all believed they faced a herculean, if not impossible, task.

Price said he was not alone in believing that, even if Selby recovered consciousness, irreparable damage to his brain, as well as his other sensitive organs, was inevitable.

Not only were many of the poisons unable to be identified due, in some cases to a complete lack of labelling, but also the quantities of each poison consumed by Leonard Selby could not be determined to any degree that would aid his treatment.

Price said that hope of recovery was so minimal that he even contacted the local police to attempt to locate Leonard Selby's next of kin and to inform them of the terrible tragedy that was being played out at his hospital.

Due to his rapidly deteriorating condition, arrangements were even initiated for Selby's body to be moved into the hospital mortuary and then for the Coroner to be notified.

Price had said that it was beyond his comprehension how Selby had survived even the first few minutes of his horrific suicide attempt and having done all that was humanly possible for Leonard Selby, all connected with the case awaited his anticipated death … minute by minute … hour by hour.

Even though Selby eventually lapsed into an even deeper coma, Price had said that, in a last desperate effort he had him placed on a life-support machine where he remained for a further four days, hovering between life and death.

Towards the end of the fourth day Price was suddenly paged within the hospital precinct to attend Leonard Selby's room immediately. He hastened to the relevant hospital wing, fully expecting that when he arrived he was merely going to be asked permission to turn off Selby's life support machine and, indeed, was somewhat annoyed that this request had not merely been conveyed to him through his mobile 'phone.

However, he was met in the corridor by a perplexed staff nurse hurrying towards him from Selby's room and was completely flabbergasted to be informed that Selby had recovered to such an extent that he had opened his eyes and even uttered a few indecipherable words to his attending nurse.

On arriving at Selby's bedside it was with complete shock and disbelief that he saw Selby's questioning bloodshot eyes turned in his direction as the staff nurse was inserting a saline drip into his left arm.

From that time onwards Selby's recovery was completely beyond his, and the other medical staff's long experience, and so very extraordinary that he felt that he should immediately inform his old colleague, Professor Quigley.

At this point in the Professor's story, and in response to my interjection asking when I could visit Leonard Selby myself, the Professor replied that Selby had already been transferred to our Cambridge complex to continue his recovery.

He had been placed within a specially designated and secure intensive care ward adjacent to the Professor's laboratory, in preparation for more detailed specialist investigation, treatment and recuperation.

The Professor added that instructions had been given that Selby's progress or deterioration needed to be meticulously recorded, around the clock, in order that all knowledge gained through his unique survival could be utilised in future treatment of patients, suffering from similar life threatening symptoms.

It was during my chat with Professor Quigley that he let slip, that in his role as the Director of the Cambridge Laboratories and the Government's unofficial advisor on germ warfare he was required to report immediately and directly to Colonel Thorpe any unusual or out of the ordinary medical case that came to his notice.

It was this same Colonel Thorpe who, some weeks later decreed that Selby's unique case had to be placed into Category 1 status of isolation and secrecy following a sudden and extremely disturbing development.

Thorpe widened his instruction to be kept informed by insisting that he should be given a written report, on a half-daily basis and contacted immediately if any significant change in Selby's medical condition arose.

These completely unprecedented interventions by Colonel Thorpe were prompted by a bizarre and tragic situation involving one of the young nurses, Jane Mather, who had been dedicatedly treating Selby's skin eruptions which, over the past week, had suddenly, and without warning manifested themselves on various areas of his arms.

We immediately prescribed high doses of an experimental antibiotic, together with a specially formulated medication to be applied directly to these two stubborn patches adjacent to his right wrist and within his right palm.

This twice daily treatment to these stubborn and painful areas was administered by this same Jane Mather, a young but very competent and experienced nurse.

It was towards the end of the week that Jane had complained to her staff nurse of feeling unwell and had been given leave to retire to her small apartment within the complex to recuperate.

Even though Jane had telephoned her closest friend Sheila, another nurse on the ward, and reported that she felt somewhat better, she asked Sheila if she would inform the Staff Nurse that she had decided, in view of her close contact with her patient Leonard Selby, to play safe and take a further day off work following a weekend's rest and recuperation.

More general concern was heightened when, on the following Tuesday, Jane failed to answer both her main flat telephone and her mobile 'phone.

When the Professor and I were alerted we both agreed with their concerns about Jane and when security eventually managed to enter her flat Jane was discovered, still in her single bed with the sightless, staring eyes of one who had suffered extreme agony in the latter stages of a lonely death.

Notwithstanding the fact that poor Jane had been dead for many hours, both the Professor and I were puzzled to notice that there were two or three extended veins, running up her left arm to her shoulder, which appeared to gently pulsating and were of a reddish hue, in direct comparison to the pale, hardly distinguishable veins, on other parts of her body.

Following this perplexing discovery, coupled with the bafflement of the reason for her death, thorough investigations of the nurse's movements were carried out, involving the close questioning of all the hospital staff that had been in close contact with either the dead nurse or her sick patient over the past five days.

Every single person, even the security staff, who had access to the nurse's flat or the wards in which she had worked, was given a rigorous medical examination in the eventuality, however remote, that further personnel had been similarly infected.

When we were completely satisfied that the infection that had killed Selby's nurse had spread no further we sat down in the Professor's office and compiled a full and comprehensive report on all matters even remotely connected to this sad episode as insisted upon by the Colonel.

The Home Office Coroner had previously been informed about her death and after some consultation between the Home Office Coroner and Colonel Thorpe, permission was finally given to transfer Jane's body to the hospital morgue after being sealed in a special sterile container, to await instructions from the Coroner about the timing of the post-mortem.

We both agreed that it was obvious that the primary investigations should be directed towards the fact that Jane Mather was in daily direct contact with her sick patient Leonard Selby. The death of this previously fit and energetic young girl could not be dismissed as purely coincidental, even without the confirmation from her forthcoming post-mortem.

All these urgent and vital questions would only be satisfied by an urgent and assiduous examination of Selby, followed by an equally meticulous and well-recorded post-mortem on Jane Mather.

Professor Quigley was also insistent, as a matter of the utmost priority, that the previously established safety regime for any persons having any contact with Selby needed to be urgently reviewed and, if found inadequate, made far more stringent, if only to ensure the utmost safety for his replacement nurse.

Only when all the full facts had been systematically reviewed, which would obviously include the findings of Jane's already scheduled autopsy, could it be established, beyond any doubt whatsoever, if Selby's infection was the cause of her demise.

We also agreed that, to reduce our patient's stress, that until the results of the autopsy were beyond doubt, Jane's continued absence should be explained, to an already increasingly concerned Selby, that her cold had turned to severe influenza and in order to reduce the risk of passing on her infection to others she had been confined to her room.

Until we were absolutely certain what had caused Jane's death, we had decreed that all visitors, hospital and support staff entering Leonard Selby's room should be required to wear the highest grade of protective clothing and comply with other related stringent safety precautions.

The Professor and I also agreed it was necessary to warn everyone involved in conducting the autopsy on Jane Mather, that the highest possible precautions were imperative during any examination of her body until her cause of death had been definitively established.

Chapter 3

DELVING INTO THE MIRE

The autopsy was conducted by the eminent Home Office pathologist, Dr. Philip Grainger, a scientist of impeccable credentials and a consummate professional and, more importantly someone in whom the Professor had the utmost faith.

All involved in the autopsy, to their expressed chagrin, had been fitted out in protective suits with an independent air supply and microphones to enable Dr. Grainger, as well as being continuously filmed, to also record in minute detail, each successive procedure as he performed his gruesome task.

This dual recording procedure, involving both voice and film, was regarded by both of us to be particularly vital in any subsequent meaningful discussion between Grainger, Professor Quigley, myself and, perhaps more crucially, Colonel Thorpe.

We professionals were completely confident that, if there was anything unusual that could have caused the nurse's death, then Dr. Grainger would discover it over the ensuing hours and could be relied upon to give his professional, dispassionate and accurate report of all matters that could have caused this girl's untimely and bizarre death.

We had previously discussed and agreed with Dr. Grainger that he should commence his work by meticulously removing the "spine like sliver" that the Professor and I had noticed, embedded in the nurses arm.

Dr. Grainger had initially objected to donning to the cumbersome protective suit with its trailing air leads but, having great respect for Professor Quigley, coupled with the Professor's absolute insistence on these unusual precautions, he had reluctantly agreed.

As we viewed the commencement of the autopsy through the thick glass windows the reason for Dr. Grainger's initial objections, to them both having to wear the suit and other safety accoutrements, became plainly obvious as their movements were slow, laboured and less precise than otherwise would have been the case.

As we all scrutinised the complex proceedings through the thick armoured glass wall of the viewing gallery, both the camera and sound levels were separately remotely controlled by two expert technicians and, as they were conveniently seated adjacent to the Professor and me, it was a simple matter for precise instructions to be given to these specially chosen operators, regarding camera angles and close-ups.

The moment that the pathologist commenced the removal of the "sliver" Professor Quigley signalled that full zoom recording should be used up to the very moment that the sample was sealed in the small glass tube.

Even to external observers It was very noticeable that, when the still vibrating "spine" had been removed from the nurse's skin by Grainger all pulsating within the distended veins of the dead nurse's left arm immediately ceased and, moreover, all her veins immediately turned to a paler hue, even to merging into her pallid dead flesh.

At a meeting later that day It was unanimously agreed, following a preliminary exchange of views with the aim of evaluating the most immediate findings of the autopsy, that the most chilling, disquieting and irrefutable revelation was that the extracted dart like "spine" appeared to be acting with a pumping operation, apparently with a life of its own.

The removal of the all the vital organs of Nurse Mather now proceeded normally, in a precise and orderly manner, with each separate organ being carefully sealed in its own specially labelled and sanitised stainless steel container, to await further detailed scrutiny.

It was then, at the request of Professor Quigley talking through the speaker into the room, that the pathologist carefully slit open the sealed plastic bag lying on the adjacent metal side table containing all Jane Mather's clothing, including her complete hospital uniform, worn on the day she had attended to Leonard Selby, prior to her feeling unwell.

Dr. Grainger, at Professor Quigley's further urgings, began to inspect each item of clothing minutely, particularly in the area of the left sleeve which coincided with the entry point of the previously removed "dart" from the nurse's arm. As he performed this procedure Dr. Grainger spoke slowly and deliberately into his microphone, remarking that a puncture mark showed clearly on the sleeve of Jane's uniform which was confirmed by the zooming in of the remotely controlled internal camera.

Following that confirmation the Professor requested Dr. Grainger if he would please look very closely at what appeared to be three or four thin streaks on the nurse's elasticated fabric waistband.

Following several minutes of careful probing with his tweezers, the pathologist noticeably gasped into his chest microphone and for the first time his professional poise momentarily slipped as he described four more miniscule, dart like "spines" to all intents and purposes very similar, if not identical, to the one he had just removed from the dead nurse's arm.

Moreover, to everyone's complete and utter bewilderment the now visibly shaken pathologist reported that all of these discarded "spines" were still exhibiting significant vibrant activity.

Later, following a more intensive analytical examination of the "spines", combined with a detailed analysis of their constituent parts, Grainger, Quigley and myself, were convinced, without any remaining element of doubt, that their deadly poisons were still virulent and lethal to any recipient.

We were half way through the filmed record of the autopsy when we were all visibly shaken when we reviewed the point where the pulsating "spine" was magnified by the camera's zoom and then returning to the section of the film showing the dead nurse's red veined lines running directly from the "spine" up her arm which, prior to the spines removal, had been regularly pulsating in a replicating rhythm.

Eventually, we all retired to our respective offices, somewhat shell shocked and drained, following the complicated and lengthy autopsy and subsequent investigations which had revealed many disturbing features, each and every one requiring more meticulous analysis before any definitive conclusion could be reached.

It had been mutually agreed, following a short discussion at the conclusion of the autopsy, that perhaps the best course of action was for Professor Quigley, myself and Dr. Grainger to each prepare his own separate dossier setting out, in as much detail as possible, his personalised particular theory, based on the mass of information recorded during the autopsy and the subsequent experiments.

Each dossier should additionally contain a personal comment firstly, on how each thought Jane Mather had met her death and secondly, how each viewed the current status of our patient, Leonard Selby when viewed in the light of all these new facts. We agreed that we would then all meet up later to compare notes.

By adopting this procedure it was then hoped that a mutually agreed format could be reached to allow us to place our concurred conclusions within one definitive report, now even more urgently demanded by Colonel Thorpe.

Chapter 4
THE CODICIL

It was some days later, when I was on the point of completing my own version of the report, when Professor Quigley burst into my room, in uncharacteristic agitation, explaining that there had been a dramatic development concerning our patient and that we should both visit him immediately.

As we hurried to the isolation ward he warned that I should be prepared for a shock in Selby's appearance, emphasising that he had already further reinforced his previous instructions to all staff that on no account whatsoever should Leonard Selby be approached without donning the full specified special protective clothing.

The sight that met our gaze through the round window of the ward door was of a nightmare scenario.

Selby's eyes were closed, his whole body visibly vibrating, with his hands and feet held by leather straps to the sides of the white metal bed and all the administering medical staff within the ward area clad in protective suits.

A series of overlapping opaque plastic curtains supported on a ceiling rail completely surrounded the bed, allowing a three foot wide walkway for the staff to gain access to their patient. In addition, there were multiple layers of the same plastic curtains forming a corridor to the ward from the security entrance, now manned by, not one, but three security guards, all dressed in similar protective clothing.

The curtains round the bed contained rectangular clear plastic windows at intervals allowing intermittent views of our patient from most positions.

In response to my query concerning the necessity for such drastic protection the Professor explained that further examination of the very detailed and video-recorded autopsy, that we had all witnessed being carried out on the dead nurse, had disclosed some alarming additional factors which had resulted in the installation of the additional elaborate curtains and other protective elements.

The Professor further explained that the autopsy had revealed that, whilst we were aware that the nurse had "a miniscule dart shaped spine or sliver of hard flesh" embedded in her arm with narrow red threads, marginally below skin depth and emanating from the point of entry, it had also been discovered that one remaining solitary pulsating vein was tracking directly from her arm to her neck and thence directly into her cranium.

This finding confirmed that, even though the nurse had been dead for some days, there was now clear and unmistakable evidence that there were some residual infected red threads in her veins that were still advancing throughout the body, clearly demonstrating how wise the Professor had been to insist that the whole autopsy had been conducted by a fully protected pathologist and his assistant.

Meeting just outside Selby's ward later that day, Professor Quigley handed me an already opened envelope which contained a letter headed "Extremely Confidential" plus an added comment that it was "For Professor Quigley's urgent and personal attention".

The contents, hurriedly hand written in Colonel Thorpe's own distinctive spidery handwriting and underlined at various sections contained one particular sentence which stood out amongst the rest giving instructions and information that …

… the nurse's body had to be preserved in strict quarantine and that he had just informed the nurse's family that, regretfully, pending the solution of certain legal matters both the Coroner's Inquest and the cremation had to be postponed indefinitely by using the excuse that further and more detailed, investigations had to be conducted to confirm the initial report of the pathologist.

As we could do no more that night we decided to revisit our patient and as we meticulously donned our protective suits complete with glass fronted headpieces in the anti-room we must have both been asking ourselves the same question? … why were Thorpe and MI6 showing such an unusual and growing interest in Selby and the dead nurse and what was the real reason behind the Inquest and funeral of Jane Mather suddenly being halted?

As we entered his ward we met a now completely lucid and apparently fully recovered Leonard Selby, his whole demeanour merely questioning the reason for our protective garb.

After carefully examining our patient, we were relieved and somewhat re-assured to find that most of the ugly blistering in many differing areas of his body had now all healed and his high fever of the previous two nights had subsided to somewhere approaching normality.

The only remaining areas of immediate concern were centred on an angry looking rash on Selby's right wrist and a similar raw red patch within his right palm.

His left eye was also somewhat bloodshot, but our joint prognosis was that this particular problem was merely due to a localised infection. Our conclusions were supported by Selby's continued insistence that his eye was not at all painful and, far more significantly, his vision appeared completely unimpaired.

Our optimism, concerning our patient's general condition, continued to increase over the next few days, which caused unforeseen consequences that would result in a tragic occurrence involving the Professor.

Selby, still apprehensive at the sight of the masked and suited attend-ants around his bed, asked us both about his whereabouts and where he was being treated and what was our joint prognosis regarding his current medical condition?

We were both convinced, by virtue of his rapid recovery that the exces-sive shaking of Selby's limbs we had all witnessed with great concern, was most likely to have been the result of the unprecedented amount of experi-mental antibiotics injected into his bloodstream to combat the residue of the poisons residing within an already fragile and damaged nervous system.

Nevertheless, on our way out the Professor telephoned the ward doc-tor to reiterate his instruction for him to be sure to remind all his staff that on no account whatsoever had any protective clothing to be removed within the vicinity of Selby. I was also aware that he later reinforced his comment by informing all staff, through a duplicated personal hand writ-ten memorandum, that this requirement to maintain protection was sacro-sanct and anyone found in contravention would be summarily dismissed.

The next day, after much debate, we paid a further joint visit to Sel-by to break the news about the death of Jane to which none of us looked forward, particularly as we had previously told him a "white lie" con-cerning her illness.

Poor Selby broke down in tears and for some minutes was inconsolable as Jane had, over the previous months, become a kind friend as well as a nurse.

Selby continued his improvement to a point that he was no longer confined to bed and was often discovered relaxing in his dressing gown, watching his television or a chosen DVD before a comforting log fire.

Leonard Selby's previous terrible skin eruptions had all disappeared leaving "pock like" marks which had responded well to the treatment I had prescribed and, even more encouragingly, had significantly reduced in size and redness. Our only remaining concern still involved the obstinate open wound within his right palm which, for some unaccountable reason, continued to defeat all our combined efforts to both diagnose and treat.

Selby' s only remaining, and quite understandable, deep concern was centred on why, if he was recovering from his infection so well, was it still necessary for visitors and everyone attending to him to continue to wear full protective clothing?

I responded by giving Selby an assurance that if his improvement continued at the same rate then, very shortly, Professor Quigley and I would most likely retract this instruction but, in the meantime, he had to realise that everyone had to be absolutely certain there was no likelihood of him inadvertently passing any infection whatsoever to his carers and other visiting staff.

Selby was still liable to be extremely upset, sometimes even moved to tears, when his nurse Jane's name was inadvertently mentioned, and on one such occasion in a consoling gesture I even placed my arm around his shoulders as I tried to reassure him with some words of comfort.

We very wisely decided against mentioning that his infection could have been in any way responsible for her death, casually suggesting that she had died from a rare case, related to pneumonia.

I now dimly recollect, just prior to our departure, that the Professor in direct contravention of his own edict, had either absentmindedly or perhaps intentionally removed the glove from his right hand and placed it over that of his patient's in a departing gesture of humanity, compassion and reassurance.

When I eventually joined Professor Quigley in the outside corridor, having both completed the complicated divesting of our protective clothing in the ward's anti-room, I could not fail to notice that he was carefully inspecting and rubbing the same hand that had gently touched Leonard Selby's only a few moments previously.

Possibly in response to my quizzical stare the Professor said that we all needed to be extremely cautious and stay professional until we had all the definitive answers concerning Leonard Selby's condition.

We both spent the remaining day minutely examining and re-examining the comprehensive results from the autopsy, followed by a microscopic examination of each sample in turn, particularly concentrating on the spines that had been recovered with such meticulous care and placed and sealed, each within their own sterile containers.

After our long and mentally tasking day, we both were looking forward to spend a well-earned night off, relaxing and dining at the local village inn but, at the very last minute, I received a call from the Professor asking to be excused as his headache, casually mentioned to me earlier in the day, had worsened and consequently felt that an early night would more advisable.

Apart from his now recovering minor eye irritation, the worst of Selby's problems appeared to be behind him and the Professor and I were encouraged in believing that we could be witnessing a truly remarkable recovery from his traumatic, albeit, self-inflicted experience.

At long last, without the distraction of the previously unremitting demands of our patient, we could both look forward to our work load returning to some essence of normality.

With Selby improving daily and consequently becoming aware that my contract at Cambridge may well be nearing completion, I was even beginning to occasionally scan the vacancy pages of the scientific and related journals in the complex's comprehensive library.

In the evenings, during our rare periods of relaxation, the Professor and I even discussed, albeit in a very general way, that we should perhaps consider producing a joint scientific paper on the whole medical history of our patient, possibly, in due course, submitting our treatise to leading medical journals for them to consider whether or not our submission merited publication.

How premature we were in making such elaborate plans was to be dramatically revealed around two weeks later by Professor Quigley, in the most unusual and bizarre circumstances.

Responding to an over vigorous knock on the door of my flat very early one morning I met a haggard and troubled looking Professor Quigley, his face pale and drawn. At my invitation he entered and flopped down in the nearest leather armchair requesting a glass of his favourite malt whisky.

After taking a sizable draught the Professor shook his head and remarked that he had been a complete fool to add, without any discussion or reference to me, a "personal codicil" to our combined final report on Leonard Selby's recovery as demanded by Colonel Thorpe.

Seeing my puzzled stare the Professor developed his comments further by explaining that, in an effort to cater for the non-scientific readers of our report, such as the Colonel, he had foolishly given an additional lay-man's view of Leonard Selby's current condition and future prospects. He explained that within his personal codicil he had mentioned the somewhat inconclusive and disturbing findings of the nurse's autopsy and that consequently he could only provide a judicious guess and not a definitive scientific explanation of Selby's condition and future prospects.

He had expanded his scientific codicil by suggesting that Selby's ingestion of the innumerable poisons into his blood stream during his suicide attempt had given him the unique capacity of producing the discovered "darts" or "slivers" containing the most lethal mixture of toxins known to man, one or more of which had most certainly been responsible for Jane Mather's death.

Moreover, he had continued in his comments, that for some unaccountable and inexplicable reason Selby's immune system had fought and naturally overcome this cocktail of self-induced infection and, as a result, had personally become completely immune to these concentrated toxins still coursing within his bloodstream.

The flow of these poisons seemed to be directed towards Leonard Selby's last remaining open wound which had continued to express itself in the tiny eruption contained within his right palm and during treatment by his nurse, Jane Mather, some of these "poisoned slivers" must have been forcibly expelled and at least one had been clearly demonstrated and proven during the autopsy, to have embedded itself in Jane's arm.

On all the available evidence, based upon his professional expertise and judgment, Jane Mather was doomed the moment the tip of the miniscule sinuous dart had touched and pierced her delicate skin.

Professor Quigley said that his "stupid and impulsive statements in his codicil" had suggested that, given the complexity and unknown number of the poisons found within the Nurse's blood sample, his considered professional opinion was that no antidote was ever likely to be produced, certainly not without decades of sophisticated and dedicated research.

Professor Quigley admitted that, in his desire to reinforce the continuing danger posed by Selby, to those who came into direct contact with him, he had made a terrible mistake in over dramatising his added report … and I quote his exact words from the document in my possession for the benefit of my listeners …

"… It appears we have within our midst a deadly human being who, whilst giving the outward appearance of a normal healthy individual, will continue to emit deadly and contagious spines from his last remaining wound within his right palm which, if touched, would be a death sentence to any unprotected contact. Leonard Selby could even be referred to as "The Human Porcupine Man". Consequently, Leonard Selby will require stringent contact management, possibly isolation, for an indeterminate length of time … possibly, even for the remainder of his life …"

When the Professor had departed I returned to my laboratory after this unsolicited and unequivocal admission of irresponsibility by my eminent colleague, with my mind in complete and utter turmoil. My feelings were aggravated by the realisation that I could not deny my own responsibilities by my abject failure to fully appreciate the danger posed by Leonard Selby to his conscientious nurse and then to personally ensure that precautions were immediately put in place to ensure her absolute protection.

After cogitating about how these unguarded, unwise comments added by my colleague could be withdrawn, I eventually decided to contact the Professor on his mobile with a view to having an urgent discussion to enable us to combine our thoughts on what was the best way forward towards ameliorating his ill-advised statement.

To my frustration my call was met with the recording that any caller should leave a message.

Some hours later, when I finally tracked the Professor down, he apologised profusely for his unavailability by explaining that he was still feeling "somewhat groggy" and had taken a few hour's nap, assuring me he was now feeling a little refreshed and indeed, had felt well enough to attend a meeting with Colonel Thorpe to discuss the veracity and implications of his naive comments and if they could be deleted in their entirety from our joint report.

He said it was remiss of him for not at least asking me if I wished to accompany him to the meeting but said he felt strongly that, as the originator of the damaging comments, he should take full responsibility and personally make every effort to mitigate the consequences of his stupid and unguarded remarks.

Quigley remarked that, to his intense disquiet, it became clear throughout his discussion with the Colonel that his added foolish comments had only served to arouse and stimulate the imagination of the Colonel.

The Professor said that Thorpe even touched on how Selby's infection might be harnessed for the benefit of the nation in some devious, but as yet undefined, manner all without any mention whatsoever of how poor Leonard Selby could be completely cured and rendered harmless to others.

Indeed the Professor related how Thorpe had theorised on how it would be possible to utilise Selby's continuing infection, even asking for his views on whether he believed that the expulsion of Selby's deadly "spines" could possibly be directed or even controlled?

We were both completely taken aback when, some days later and part way through a hastily called meeting with the Colonel, we were introduced to an American Secret Service Agent, a Frank Shelton who, supported by a laptop computer and portable screen, embarked on an hour long lecture on the various options that were open to Great Britain and the USA to deal with the leaders of the various factions that had been classed as "enemies of the state".

Frank Shelton was a balding man of medium stature with an air of competence and authority only to be expected from a senior member of the CIA and, as such, was obviously a man to be taken extremely seriously.

Shelton, continued, that over the past eighteen months there had been meetings and internet exchanges at the very highest level between the security services of our two countries, in an attempt to explore and rationalise the best way to combat the terrorist organisations that were creating such havoc for America, Great Britain and its Allies worldwide.

He emphasised that all parties were becoming desperate to find some solution that would stem the unremitting proliferation of these multifarious organisations.

There had been particular emphasis, within these highly confidential exchanges, to explore any means whatsoever that could lead to the elimination of the leaders of all these organisations, without endangering the populous within which they were operating ... leaders who were not beyond using women and children as human shields.

There were some who thought that the current indiscriminate bombing operations by many countries were having the negative effect of actually encouraging some ideologically confused and disenchanted youth to join these organisations that the bombing was meant to disrupt and destroy.

Hence the reason why research, on both sides of the Atlantic, was now intensified to explore alternative and more sophisticated, scientific and selective methods of assassinating the leaders of these groups, in other words "Cutting the Heads off the Hydra!".

Shelton touched on one line of research which he explained was being currently pursued in his country, America, which caused each person around the table to look at each other in a combination of disbelief and not a little amusement.

He postulated upon the distinct possibility of employing remotely operated, highly sophisticated drones which Shelton said could eventually be programmed to detect the unique heartbeat of the targeted person and then the device would be deployed eliminating the chosen victim, without harming any innocent bystanders.

However, seeing the scepticism etched on all his audience's faces, including Colonel Thorpe's he had to acknowledge, that even based on the most optimistic forecasts, it could be many years before such a device was perfected, if ever, and everyone accepted that the problem was here and now and as a consequence, time was of the essence.

Frank Shelton concluded his talk by dropping a diplomatic bombshell on his audience by stating that his security services had now agreed with its British counterpart that they both should now be vigorously exploring to find out if Leonard Selby could be utilised as a "visiting assassin" by infecting his selected victims by personal contact.

It was even feasible and not beyond the bounds of possibility that the living deadly "spines" that were still being continuously emitted by Leonard, could be carefully harvested and by some means ensured that they were handled by a recipient target, with the significant likelihood of infection and inevitable death.

If this could be accomplished then it would even completely eliminate the requirement, combined with the accompanying risk, for personal contact by Leonard Selby with his intended victim.

When Shelton took his seat to the accompanying assenting murmurs of his audience, led by a smiling Colonel Thorpe, the Professor and I looked at each other, barely disguising the revulsion and disgust of what we had been told.

We were just two against the room and, in vain, we both made rigorous objections to any suggestion that our patient should be even envisaged as a tool of MI6 and the CIA, finally imploring all present to remember that they too had a duty of trust and care to our patient.

It was at that crucial meeting when Colonel Thorpe laid bare his inner thoughts for the first time. He said that he truly believed that Leonard Selby's unique infection offered the countries fighting the Islamic State and their Allies a unique, deadly and selective method of assassination, coupled with the great advantage that from the time of a target's infection certain death could ensue many months later

It was pointed out that, due to the long period elapsing between infection, illness and death it would allow Leonard Selby to depart the scene without any vestige of suspicion being aroused. Consequently, he could be deployed time and time again in his role of National assassin.

Experiments had confirmed that victims would fatally succumb to being infected, many weeks, even months later, thus ensuring that there was a minimal chance of any death being connected to a previous visit to the area by Leonard Selby.

Thorpe sternly warned all present that no minutes, even notes, of this meeting should be made and all discussions concerning Selby's

death-dealing potential should be strictly restricted to those persons pres-
ent concluding by reminding everyone that they were each bound by the
Official Secrets Act.

Finally he reiterated that, not only was Selby now viewed as a fea-
sible weapon of assassination by MI6, but also by the highest echelons
within the CIA.

Colonel Thorpe further warned that, for the avoidance of doubt, from
this day onwards all matters concerning Leonard Selby were sheltered
under the umbrella of utmost secrecy and furthermore, before anyone
would be allowed to leave the meeting room each would have to sign
their full compliance.

As the meeting broke up, the Professor and I, even though we had
both penned our signatures to the Form of Agreement that had been passed
round, remained rooted to our seats, our thoughts paralysed by the ulti-
mate realisation that our patient had been enrolled, without his acquies-
cence or any meaningful debate, as a State controlled assassin.

As we drove back to our laboratory the Professor wearily added he very
much feared that our patient had been snatched from our care and pro-
tection.

It was when we arrived at the complex the following morning that
our concerns were validated by the sight of additional uniformed guards
and new personnel arriving at the complex.

Revised orders were immediately implemented and an exclusion zone
around Leonard Selby's accommodation block ensured that we were both
denied our hitherto unrestricted access.

At this point in his story George Deakin took the opportunity
for a well-earned break after his long day at his desk.

Feeling the desire for some clean fresh air, he donned and half
zipped up his Barbour jacket as he strolled through his somewhat neglected rear garden and noticing his greenhouse had some
broken panes and his boundary contained some rotting leaning
fence posts, he was reminded that, for over one year his whole
life had been taken over from the commonplace, leaving him lit-

tle time for normal pursuits. He surveyed the mist covered panorama down through the scattered tall pine trees and listened to the intermingled woodland sounds, enhanced in clarity by the eerie stillness of the early evening air.

Towards the end of his gentle walk the song birds grew increasingly silent due to the imminent approach of dusk, which encouraged the increasing numbers of bats swirling about in the semi-darkness.

George felt more relaxed as he embraced the multitude of other intermittent woodland noises, all blending in with the sound of the strongly flowing adjacent stream, its usual soft murmurings now greatly accentuated by the effect of recent heavy and prolonged storms.

George's musings were suddenly jerked back to reality!

Shivering in the night air, he slowly fully zipped up his jacket against the cold breeze and running his fingers through his thinning hair he somewhat gingerly stretched his aching back and arms that were feeling the effects of his recent hours of bending over his dictation machine.

With a resigned sigh George turned on his heels walked back to his cabin and finally entered the welcoming warm glow of the interior, feeling refreshed and more able to continue his daunting, but essential labours.

After a hurried, minimal snack of cold chicken legs, bread and butter followed by a wedge of moist parkin, all finally washed down by a quenching cold apple juice, he sat down at his table to continue recording his incredible story.

He, more than most, fully appreciated that no matter how long it took, his warning message needed to contain each and every minute detail of his over year-long nightmare.

The requirement, to disclose the whole detailed scenario of his months of torment, was absolutely essential if his appeal had the slightest chance in ever convincing any of its recipients to take his warnings seriously and, even more importantly, have the courage to act.

The difficult part even for a convinced person was to take that first courageous step towards exposing to the world the catastrophic path to mayhem, currently being planned by the fanatical megalomaniacs ... Colonel Thorpe and his entourage.

George Deakin was placing his trust in his fellow man, or woman, that all his warnings would not be in vain!

Stretching his arms once more and leaning forward, he pressed the recorder's starter button to continue his narrative ...

Chapter 5

THE PROFESSOR'S DILEMMA

It was the following morning when I called on the Professor, with the sole intent of discussing in far greater depth, the disturbing consequences of that truly horrendous meeting with Colonel Thorpe and the American CIA boss.

It was also my intention to endeavour to alleviate the Professor's obvious distress and concern that he, personally, had handled matters badly and thereby had inadvertently placed the life of his patient, Leonard Selby and even perhaps our own, at greater risk.

During our lengthy, detailed and at times personal discussions we touched upon the whole scenario before us, ranging from the time that his friend and colleague Brian Price had introduced a very sick Leonard Selby to the Professor's care, straight through to the horrendous situation that currently prevailed.

It became clear to me, as our talk progressed, that the Professor's original professional and clinical relationship, which normally and properly exists between physician and patient, had been gradually eroded to a dangerous point.

Leonard Selby had become more of a friend than a patient.

My own relationship with Selby had been similarly affected which allowed me to more easily understand and excuse the Professor's current dilemma.

Such a dramatic change in our relationships was a natural and understandable result of many months of unremitting daily visits, treatment and care, involving just one patient.

The more the Professor talked the more he disclosed that his close and prolonged relationship with Selby had resulted in him dangerously overstepping the normally accepted boundary between doctor and patient.

This had inevitably first clouded, and then undermined his normally, impeccable judgment, which had unfortunately resulted in his unwise codicil to what was originally intended to comprise our joint low-key and balanced report to Colonel Thorpe.

The Professor confessed that it pained him to think that he had betrayed his responsibility of duty and care through his unguarded comments which he had inserted at the end of, what was supposed to have been our joint and mutually agreed report and which we both realised could now never be retracted.

The strain on the Professor's face was apparent and completely understandable but I was not to know, until towards the end of our long discussion, that the visible disintegration in his poise and demeanour was not restricted to just one single cause.

I will remember, to my dying day, that it was nearing the end of our discussion that he first allowed me a view of his inflamed wrist and the red, extended vein-like threads disappearing past his shoulder upwards towards his neck.

Any further comment by me, at that particular moment in time, would have been superfluous, for we both chillingly recognised that his symptoms exactly replicated the symptoms of Nurse Jane Mather, viewed by all those present during the autopsy on the poor nurse, some weeks previously.

Professor Quigley now did not need to remind me of the occasion during our visit to Leonard Selby when he had foolishly, and in contravention of his own implicit instructions, instinctively removed one of his protective gloves in order to place his bare hand on Selby's, in a gesture of compassion and consolation in an effort to reassure his distressed patient.

I now understood far more clearly why, on our way out from that particular visit, he had reiterated so vehemently, his previous implicit instructions that all visiting and attending staff needed remain fully and totally protected when they were anywhere within the proximity of Leonard Selby.

When he had rolled down his sleeve and replaced his jacket Professor Quigley sternly ordered me that I should, say and do nothing, adding that he was sure that he could affect a cure to his problem.

In response to my obvious scepticism and concern, he explained that he had already injected some of Leonard Selby's blood into his own bloodstream and confidentially expected that the antibodies, contained in our patient's blood, would eventually help his own immune system to successfully fight against his own infection.

Noticing my air of disbelief, he assured me he was already aware of some slight reduction in redness within the inflamed veins in his arm and, with great reluctance, I gave him my promise to comply with his request, at least until we met again the next day.

I then departed, depending upon the Professor's firm assurance he would contact me first thing in the morning to discuss and deliberate upon some possible avenues towards some further alternative treatment for his condition.

Sadly, this was the last discussion I ever had with my eminent colleague.

During the night, when presumably his condition must have suddenly deteriorated, he had contacted the attending night-ward doctor who decided, rather than telephone me, to pass on the shocking news directly to Colonel Thorpe.

The Colonel left a curt message on my answerphone, coldly stating that the Professor had suddenly been taken ill in the night and was under treatment at another hospital.

The Colonel was obviously completely unaware I had visited the Professor the previous evening and that I was fully aware of seriousness of his symptoms.

It is now my firm understanding, following my own intensive and covert enquiries, that the Professor was immediately moved, at Colonel Thorpe's personal instruction, by a private ambulance to an unknown destination.

Certainly, to my best knowledge, the Professor had not been treated within any ward within the complex or possibly even within the county of Cambridge and the night-ward doctor was obviously under strict instructions not to speak of the matter to anyone.

Being fully aware of my deep regard for Professor Quigley and my increasing despair about his wellbeing Colonel Thorpe merely responded by adamantly denying me any access to the Professor and then even categorically refusing to discuss, either the Professor's present location or even his state of health.

This obduracy by Thorpe reinforced my conviction that the Professor had died, or perhaps even been lethally injected, very shortly after he was moved from his apartment in the Cambridge complex. Whatever occurred, I can categorically state that his death was certainly not following the reported intense fire at his London home. I am more than ever convinced, beyond any doubt whatsoever, that Professor Quigley was Leonard Selby's unintentional second victim, following the earlier demise of his nurse, Jane Mather!

I would have thought that the Colonel would have had the good grace to allow me at least the weekend to mourn the death of my mentor who had become, over the relatively brief period I had known him, not only my esteemed professional colleague, but also a good friend and confidant.

However, this was not to be, for some days prior to the Professor's funeral I was asked, or rather instructed, by Colonel Thorpe to accompany him the very next day to see Leonard Selby, domiciled within his well-guarded isolation block.

Thorpe had insisted, due to my long association with Leonard Selby that he required me to accompany him to break the news of the Professor's sudden demise, insisting that no other details should be given to Leonard, apart from the fact that he had died in a tragic fire at his London home.

Due to the fact that my only knowledge, concerning the Professor's death, was confined to the newspaper reports at the time, the Coroner's verdict and the Colonel's continued intransigence to discuss any other possible cause, I was in no position to challenge the universally accepted explanation.

I still remember the whole drawn out ghastly funeral proceedings, not only for the platitudes and eulogies from academics and others who were completely unknown to me, and possibly to the Professor, but even more for the incongruous, inscrutable men in black overcoats, equipped with earphones who vainly attempted to merge with the bemused grieving relatives, the congregation and curious onlookers, mingling both inside and outside the church, before during and at the conclusion of the service.

One of these expressionless, taciturn men ushered me in and out of one of the three official cars, all standing out with their brown tinted windows and so patently not any part of the formal family cortège.

The Colonel even, in spite of my protestations, persuaded me against speaking personally to the family and offering my condolences, mumbling some garbled nonsense about being concerned about my personal safety due to my special knowledge of working with the Professor and Leonard Selby.

The facts surrounding the Professor's death were never again mentioned in my presence and the whole sycophantic charade surrounding the funeral still sickens me ... but it also had the effect of awakening concerns about my own fragile predicament by being "expendable", should I ever think of stepping over the official line ... the Colonel's completely inflexible and very fine line!

Listening to Thorpe and his subordinate's in his office, a mere three days following the funeral, eulogising on his crusade to protect the nation from all tyrants, dictators and other forms of demagogues, at all costs and by every means within his power, I was left in no doubt concerning the Colonel's aims and inflexible mind set.

He also left me in no doubt that he had the full backing and support of some very influential members of the UK Government and, perhaps more significantly, the undiminished support and endorsement of a significant number of leading members of the American CIA.

Moreover, Thorpe and his cabal were now obviously completely convinced that they had, in the person of poor Leonard Selby, a "killing tool" in their possession that could rid the world of all those fanatical leaders continually encouraging atrocities in many areas of the World.

The Colonel took every available opportunity to pressurise me into being a "fully paid up member" of his crusade by finally accepting his premise that, in Leonard Selby, the West had been presented with the perfect assassin who, when managed by his minders, would be capable of making the world a safer and better place for all freedom loving people.

He appeared absolutely oblivious to the clear fact that, he and his fellow travellers were also ruthless and fanatical towards achieving their own aims.

His tirade was frightening and only served to reveal his ultimate aim of gaining absolute control of Leonard Selby, in both mind and body.

Perhaps realising that he had betrayed too much of his naked ambitions, the Colonel abruptly brought the conversation around to explain my special and particularised role in his maniacal scheme, emphasising that it was imperative that Selby was persuaded to view me more as a friend and confidant rather than merely his medical practitioner. The Colonel even attempted to flatter my ego by expressing the view that, since the death of Professor Quigley, I was now the only professionally qualified person left who could successfully supervise the course of treatment for his malady that would eventually lead Selby towards a full and sustainable recovery.

My whole being felt numb and sickened at the full realisation of what I had so innocently agreed to become part of, so many months previously, during my initial meeting with Professor Quigley at the Colonnade Hotel.

Thorpe, with his arm around my shoulders, then began to quietly and systematically fill in the missing details of his scheme, solely aimed towards the ruthless manipulation of Selby through convincing him that his role and contribution to his country was to fully co-operate in the perfection and implementation of his death dealing gift.

He emphasised that the task that lay ahead for me was to whole heartedly endorse the efforts of his entourage of mind-bending specialists, to slowly and gradually build upon Leonard Selby's already firmly established belief that the death of his son and that of his dear wife, were indisputably and inarguably caused by the persons and organisations contained on the "Thorpe hit list".

My role, he insisted, was absolutely imperative in persuading Selby to co-operate in becoming a loyal and subservient assassin under his personal direction.

My revulsion reached a new low when he casually implied that Honours and financial security could inevitably flow to all concerned if there was a successful outcome to the horrific scenario that he relentlessly laid before me, hour by hour, day by day and week by week.

On one hand I felt completely trapped by this ruthless, dangerous megalomaniac but, on the other hand, I simultaneously realised that I needed to play for time until I could safely warn the outside world about this monstrous and obscene employment of a human killing machine ... ostensibly in his country's name.

I realised that my own life was precariously balanced, now that I was in possession of his complete agenda involving Leonard Selby, should he even harbour the slightest suspicion that I intended to expose his plans to the World.

I decided that my best course of action was to continue in my deputed role and by so doing gain his trust and in the meantime explore some way to elude his unremitting twenty-four hour surveillance and control.

By maintaining this complicated façade I eventually gained the feeling that it had convinced the obviously unhinged and unpredictable Colonel that I now appreciated his reasons for manipulating Selby and moreover that I had finally accepted that the end could justify the means ... and that those means ... the Colonel's objectives ... coincided with the National interest.

Whether or not Colonel Thorpe was fully convinced in my loyalty I will never know because, when talking in his office prior to our daily visit to Leonard Selby, our conversation was interrupted by the sudden entry of one of his security men who whispered in Thorpe's ear.

When the man had left the room Thorpe explained that he had just received information that Selby was now much calmer and being prepared for our visit.

We set off down the corridor towards Selby's isolation ward, entering by the glass cubical built just outside the entrance to his room which held a small desk at which were seated his two impassive guards.

I was handed an iris identification scanner and, somewhat bizarrely, even Colonel Thorpe, was required to satisfy this scanner prior to being allowed to enter through the air-sealed doors.

Leonard Selby was relaxing reading a magazine, seated on a leather settee in the corner of his warm and comfortable well-furnished lounge. His self-contained apartment also included a large bedroom, a small kitchen-diner, leading to a well-appointed bathroom.

His minimal furnishings comprised a television cabinet, some audio equipment and DVD Player on a small mahogany table in a corner. There were also several unusual features that set the room apart from the normal bed-sit, not least were two large openings, set at equally spaced intervals, glazed with sand-blasted glass blocks which limited the extent to which daylight could enter the room.

At the far end was a six foot square window, glazed with what appeared to be thick bullet proof glass, through which the gardens below could be viewed and emphasising the room's claustrophobic atmosphere, this was the one and only window that allowed Selby any glimpse of the outside world.

Taking up one complete wall a viewing gallery had recently been installed, fitted with three twelve-inch diameter steel framed windows at regular intervals through which Selby could be kept under constant observation. Every one of these portholes had been fitted with one-way glass to enable any person within the gallery to discreetly observe Selby, without disturbing him at any time of the day or night.

Yet another striking and unique feature of the room was a large white metal unit embedded in the ceiling from which emitted a continuous soft whirring noise, presumably containing some sophisticated air-filtering unit to maintain negative air pressure within the suite of rooms, as an additional safeguard against any possible escaping infection.

Colonel Thorpe signalled for the electric door leading directly from the viewing gallery into the apartment to be opened and he gestured to me to precede him into the room.

George Selby, his attention drawn by the humming electrics of the gallery door, glanced towards us and smiling, waving his un-protected left hand in greeting.

Since the incident involving the Professor inadvertently touching Selby's right wrist, which everyone was convinced had caused the infection and which had led to his subsequent death, I had insisted that his right palm should be covered at all times apart from when he was receiving treatment from his personal nurse.

Some weeks prior to his death, the Professor and I had both agreed that whilst the palm wound was the only remaining source that offered any significant danger of infection to his visitors the specially designed and sophisticated protection to this area also ensured that the daily treatment offered by his, specially trained, replacement nurse, would be able to be undertaken in absolute safety.

This innovative protection to Selby's hand also had the added advantage of eliminating the need for staff and visitors to don any protective clothing.

Selby obviously had an excellent rapport with his replacement nurse Amanda and, after exchanging some further niceties, I quietly explained that the Colonel and I had just dropped in to see him for a general chat and at the same time, hopefully, provide answers to any remaining questions or concerns that he still harboured about his predicament.

Notwithstanding my misgivings about my new role, following my earlier meeting with Thorpe, I patiently and methodically explained to Selby that, in my opinion, he was finally out of personal danger from his life-threatening infection but I cautioned that his remaining open wound on his palm still required constant treatment and meticulous monitoring by his nurse.

Over the next days and weeks the infection emanating from Selby's palm was regularly checked and the findings confirmed, beyond any doubt, and to everyone's amazement, not least my own, that his palm wound still remained virulent.

Weeks became months and, it was with increasing difficulty, that I continued my pretence of fully supporting the malevolent objectives of Colonel Thorpe and his entourage, whilst simultaneously searching for any slight chink that I could exploit within the unremitting security system that now pervaded and controlled my whole existence within the confines of the Cambridge complex.

Even though I was never informed officially, I was certain that my entire flat had been placed under "round the clock" surveillance including recently installed concealed cameras and microphones following my awareness that my flat had been entered in my absence.

One late evening, whilst enjoying a rare occasion of relaxation by watching an absorbing television drama, there was a demanding ring at my door and the security observation screen clearly showed Colonel Thorpe, accompanied by a complete stranger, standing in the soft glow of my porch light.

After pulling up my loosened tie and slipping on my jacket, I pressed the control button allowing entry and, when their overcoats had been stowed in the hall vestibule, Thorpe introduced his companion as Mr. Sebastian Standish.

Standish was a well dressed, gaunt middle-aged man with the bearing of one who expected to be obeyed without question, completely devoid of the slightest charm or any propensity to engage in small talk.

I was somewhat surprised that, for the first time since our acquaintance, Colonel Thorpe appeared somewhat subservient, even to the point of demurring to his obviously senior colleague.

Speaking in staccato phrases, Standish came straight to the point by insisting that I needed to be fully acquainted with the fast moving scenario concerning my patient.

He reiterated Thorpe's message by emphasising that, following Professor Quigley's death, I was the obvious choice to instil in my patient that he now had a moral duty to repay all the long and enormously expensive care he had received from the State which had virtually brought him back from the dead.

Sebastian Standish, his steel blue eyes boring into mine, insisted that I needed to finally accept that it was in everyone's interests, not least my patient's, that I willingly agreed to be actively engaged in the programme that had been meticulously devised by him and his American counterpart's medical experts.

The programme had been devised with the sole aim of converting Leonard Selby into mental submission.

Laying a hand on my shoulder he assured me that the procedures which had been designed by a select team of British and American psychologists would be as non-invasive as possible. Their emphasis would be on manipulating Leonard Selby's already fragile mental state, with the aim of slowly building upon his already deep seated conviction that the deaths of his cherished son and beloved wife were caused by the same persons and leaders of organisations that he was now being asked to eliminate.

All the smooth talking, packaged into psychological jargon, could not disguise the fact that my patient was going to be "brainwashed" into becoming a killing machine, within the guise of patriotism!

Continuing in the same vein, Standish informed me that it had been decided, again at the very highest level, that Leonard Selby was potentially an extremely important and valuable weapon that could, in the pres-

ent volatile international environment, be utilised for the benefit of his country and its allies.

I was completely taken aback by Standish disclosing, for the first time, that he had the full and unequivocal backing of no less a person than the Home Secretary who, he confirmed, had personally sanctioned whatever it took to indoctrinate poor Leonard Selby.

Having seen, and experienced at first hand, the extent and sophistication by which the whole complex was guarded, all mobile 'phones having being confiscated and all the other telephone calls monitored around the clock, even if I had wished, there was no way that I could have exposed this developing and disturbing situation to the outside world.

If I was ever to expose the miscreants and prevent the escalation of their schemes the only remaining solution open to me was to engineer my escape from the complex without delay!

After a short and uncomfortable tea break, during which Standish was engaged in a prolonged conversation on his mobile, presumably with some underling, he eventually returned to continue his tirade.

He did not disguise the fact that it had already been decided, at the very highest level, that if Selby could be successfully engineered into a willing participant, the authorities would not hesitate to deploy him without delay.

The Colonel added that their decision was completely justified by the fact that all democracies were fighting a battle for survival that had to be won by utilising every possible advantage in their armoury. Standish, his grey piercing eyes still looking straight into my own, asked me outright if I had any possible conception of what advantage any State or Country would possess if they had a person, such as Selby, who could be trained to unleash certain death towards another chosen person by no other means than personal contact, even perhaps, just a mere handshake?

More recent experiments, Standish enthusiastically continued, had shown the time of certain death, after contact, took an indeterminate period, varying between some weeks or even months. This varying time scale, he continued, was another huge advantage, due to the impossibility of linking a death to any previous date of contact.

Moreover, it had been definitively proven, by his medical team, that the root cause of such infection and the victim's certain death would defy even the most thorough and intensive autopsy and consequently would most likely be assumed to be due to some very rare form of sepsis or septicaemia.

Chillingly, Standish's eyes seemed to gleam with relish at the very thought of such power at his disposal, with the Colonel at his side still nodding in mute approval.

Standish then reiterated, what Colonel Thorpe had already mentioned during an earlier meeting with me so many months ago, that by a unique quirk of fate, the Democratic world was potentially, now in possession of a means to fatally infect any chosen human target with certainty and absolute impunity.

He demonstrated his complete and utter conviction to the cause by emphatically stating that the elimination of these carefully chosen individuals would remove, at a stroke, their demonic influence on their growing vulnerable young followers. The removal of these fanatics would result in the saving of millions of innocent lives through preventing conflicts and would, concurrently, make the world a better and safer place for future generations.

With his penetrating eyes demonstrating far more than words, the man's absolute conviction in his belief that Selby could be his agent of death, sent shivers through my whole being ...

... Surely George, he said, spreading out his hands towards me, this is the ultimate example of the end justifying the means?

But we need to be assured! ... Are you with us or against us?

Bereft of any rational retort I meekly responded by asking how he could be certain that Selby, in his already fragile mental state, would suddenly and without warning not go amok, rip off his hand protection and infect the innocent, not least his nurses and other staff attending to his daily needs.

Standish was dismissive, even scathing in his response by emphasising that, when his team, of which I should remember I was now a vital part, had completed their programmed psychotherapy of Leonard Selby he would be more obedient than his pet dog.

I foolishly commented that, sometimes even the most docile of dogs have been known to bite their owner.

With undisguised annoyance at my somewhat puerile remark, Standish suddenly stood up, straightened and without even shaking my hand curtly nodded to Colonel Thorpe at the same time coldly stating that they should take their leave ... as they made their way to the car Colonel Thorpe turned, just as I was on the point of closing my front door, and barked instructions that I should attend a meeting at 10.00 am the next morning to discuss the detailed programming of Leonard Selby.

Standish curtly added, what I took to be an unambiguous warning, that he would brook no failure on my part ... I was to attend as instructed, co-operate fully or suffer the consequences adding, in a more conciliatory, but non-the-less sinister tone ...

"George we really need you to be part of the team ... what is more, your country deserves your full and committed assistance in this national emergency ... Leonard Selby trusts you as a friend and is surely entitled to your full and unequivocal support".

Whilst closing the front door on my visitors I viewed Colonel Thorpe, outlined in the dim glow of the porch lamp, half turning towards me and gesturing in a resigned manner before following Standish towards where the black Ministry car was already purring its readiness in the cold night air.

The next morning at exactly 8.00 am my bedside telephone shrilled its command to awake and a woman's monotone voice at the other end reminded me of the impending 9.40 am car pick up for our 10.00 o'clock appointment in the complex's conference room.

At precisely 9.40 am I was sped towards the complex and, following the usual identity checks by the taciturn security guards, I entered the conference room to meet the penetrating gaze of Sebastian Standish standing alongside the Colonel.

They introduced me to three complete strangers, one, it was explained, was a senior figure in the American diplomatic service called Harry accompanied by Graham and Todd. The trio greeted me, with obvious American accents, and it was briefly explained that they were on special secondment to British intelligence.

To my best recollection, their surnames were never disclosed and in my current state of mind I was not inclined to ask, but over the next twenty minutes, fortified by copious jugs of strong coffee and tasteless digestive biscuits, I was subjected to a further bombardment of facts and figures reinforcing the grave and ever increasing dangers to Great Britain, America and their Allies following the twin towers disaster by Al-Qaeda, Boko Haram, al-shabab, the rapidly growing problem of ISIS and finally the al-Muhajiroun, who had targeted the United Kingdom as far back as 1997.

They were unanimous in their view that the prime cause of all the subsequent ferment that was currently being inflicted upon the world was the disastrous Iraq War which had unleashed the disastrous sectarian civil war in Iraq between Kurd, Sunni and Shia finally resulting in the complete alienation of the Iraq Shia dominated government. These inter-racial divisions had always existed but had been kept in check, albeit by dubious and, to some, totally unacceptable restraining methods by Saddam Hussein.

His restraining, albeit ruthless influence, had been completely underestimated and misjudged by George Bush and Tony Blair who had each obtained a majority vote in their parliaments for war on statements mainly based on the existence of "weapons of mass destruction", which later had been proved to be completely false.

The resulting American led invasion of Iraq, supported by the UK, exposed these divisions within Iraq, recently given new life by the conflict in Syria which in turn provided impetus to the aims of the Islamic State infecting the whole region.

I was subjected to their relentless bombardment, itemising the increasing threats emanating from current Middle Eastern leaders, heads of terrorist organisations and even Yemen's Shia-Houthi and North Korea was not left out of the equation.

Finally, they concentrated on the increasing attacks in France within Jewish areas, the supermarket bombings and the massacre at publishing house of Charlie Hebdo.

Surely, Standish repeated, echoed in unison by his colleagues, millions of people marching and demonstrating against these terrorists and their despotic aims could not be wrong?

Myriads of examples of attacks, methods and threats by each and every one of these evil organisations were thrown at me until I felt that I, and not my patient, was becoming the subject of their brainwashing techniques.

Even in my own mentally battered state I was fully aware of their main aim, which was to persuade me that their cause was just and to gain my unreserved support towards their Machiavellian scheme to manipulate Leonard Selby to become subservient.

Moreover, the vulnerability of Russia was not ignored by mentioning the Islamic threats against Radio Echo of Moscow for publicising the result of their poll showing that 70 % of their listeners believed that the Russian media should republish the cartoons depicting the Prophet Muhammad.

Internationally known hate figures were banded about that morning as they claimed that they had indisputable knowledge that all on their hit list were currently plotting the downfall of the free world, both openly and covertly.

The three Americans emphasised the activities of Boko Haram in Nigeria and the surrounding countries involving the killing women and children and lying waste to vast areas of many countries.

Standish bizarrely even brought Hitler and his cronies into their argument by hypothesising how the Second World War could have been prevented if such a weapon as Leonard Selby had existed in the late thirties to infect and kill these evil men before they could lay waste Europe and kill countless millions of innocent people.

Colonel Thorpe then asked me a direct question, which even now I find difficult to fault or deny ... is it not better to employ this "Heaven sent" method of undermining and finally eliminating all these vicious regimes than go along the previously taken route of Afghanistan and Iraq, which inevitably had led to the destruction of the innocent population's whole infrastructure, exacerbated the displacement and resulting misery of huge numbers of refugees and sacrificing the lives of many of our and other deployed armed forces?

We now have means to accomplish those aims in the form of Leonard Selby and we need to know that you are either for or against us?

Standish interjected at this point by stating that everyone was fully aware that any botched attempt at assassination by conventional means, even if successful, would be catastrophic and would inevitably exposed the perpetrators and their allies to the wrath of world opinion and most likely would be avenged by the successors of those assassinated.

It was obvious that all Thorpe's clique were absolutely convinced that, in Leonard Selby, they had, by an incredible quirk of fate, been handed a potentially perfect killing machine, and it only remained for Leonard Selby to be convinced to co-operate and thus avenge his wife and son.

Even to this day I must reluctantly admit that even I was very nearly convinced by their arguments … my progress towards complete and utter capitulation was only stemmed by a remaining flicker of moral concern which thankfully increased as each day progressed.

I now admit, to my unremitting shame, that my fears in the guise of self-preservation, overcame all my moral reservations by my finally agreeing to use whatever influence I had with Leonard Selby to assist in training him to become that ultimate assassin … The Porcupine Man!

Apart from basic self-preservation, already given as my pathetic excuse for acquiescing to their demands, as a scientist I do readily concede that I was not a little intrigued and fascinated by the possibility of a person being successfully programmed to kill on command.

My understandable fear for my own safety, coupled with this intense scientific curiosity, eventually won the battle over my conscience.

I was intrigued by what mind-bending methodology would be employed by Thorpe and Standish's psychologists to induce a previously peace-loving and vulnerable private citizen to eventually agree to become a lethal tool, albeit in the service of his country.

I can still hardly bear to admit, even in this recording, my own part in the proceedings that took place over the next few months, possibly due to the dawning realisation that I might have been the victim of a type of brainwashing myself by being persuaded, against all my natural instincts, that it was in Leonard Selby's best interests to have by his side a trusted friend who he could confide in throughout his unremitting ordeal.

Thankfully, possibly due in no small part to both Standish's and Thorpe's lingering suspicion regarding my complete loyalty to the operation, my involvement was confined to the role of friend and confidant to Selby. However, even as a mere supporting observer, I felt extreme unease and a growing concern towards my patient's mental state as the process of mind grooming developed.

Thankfully, Selby's general physical health became less of a concern and the pockmarks which had covered his entire body in the very early stages of his illness had now faded to the point of invisibility, likewise his previously inflamed face and neck had recovered to a point which now allowed normal daily shaving.

The originally designed protection covering his right hand had now been replaced by a bespoke moulded plastic lockable device which could only be released by authorised medical staff.

Within this protection was a removable pad and the continuous chemical analysis of the spines obtained from this source unequivocally demonstrated to my concern, but to the obvious delight and unashamed satisfaction of Thorpe and Standish, the unremitting lethal nature of the "deadly spines" being continuously ejected from his palm wound.

My own view, supported by the other consultants, was that the poisons, that had killed both the nurse and the Professor, would remain virulent and continue to be expelled through this minute open wound until all the poisons within his blood stream had been significantly weakened by his own unique immune system.

Considering the massive dosage of multiple poisons that Leonard Selby had miraculously survived during his abortive suicide attempt, the period calculated for the continued emission of these deadly "spines", even though decreasing in quantity, could most likely be measured in many months, if not years.

Apart from the protective cover to his right hand, Leonard Selby would have appeared to any layman to be a perfectly normal patient, merely recuperating from a mild illness.

Now that his condition had finally stabilised and the protection to his hand had been perfected, the device allowed all his doctors, nurses and visitors freedom to come and go completely without any protective clothing. This had the further advantage of bolstering everyone's confidence, not least his own, regarding his prospects for eventually regaining his full health and vigour.

Chapter 6

THE SLOUGH OF DESPOND

It was late one evening some weeks later during conducting some experiments in my laboratory when, prior to returning to my flat, I had the sudden and completely inexplicable urge to observe my patient's demeanour when he was completely relaxed and unaware he was being watched.

I was becoming increasingly concerned about his state of mind and how he was coping with his relative isolation coupled with the almost continuous "brainwashing techniques" to which he was being subjected.

To observe Selby, on a pretext of retrieving a document from my office, I managed to surreptitiously enter the unlit one-way glass viewing gallery and sat quietly and observed him through the portholes as he viewed his television.

Being assured that he was not showing any obvious signs of stress and deprivation I was on the point of leaving my dark vantage point when I became a witness to a completely unexpected and bizarre event. Leonard Selby turned off his television and strolled over to stand staring out of his solitary window which presented a panoramic view to the illuminated rain lashed lawns and gale twisting trees far below his third floor room.

Suddenly, his telephone must have rung out and after a short conversation he answered with a nod of his head and thoughtfully replaced the receiver.

I noticed with puzzlement that he was in the act of removing his hand protection when suddenly, presumably hearing a knock, he stood and faced the door and it was then that I noticed Standish and a tall, bearded white coated stranger.

I was to learn later that this stranger was a consultant Psychologist, Professor Wright, who was attached to the prison service. Wright entered Selby's room ahead of Sebastian Standish, both closely followed by three more strangers, middle-aged men, all clad in similar white coats.

The latter three all had abnormally pale complexions, coupled with an undefinable air of insecurity, in complete contrast to the immaculately dressed Standish and his impressive bearded companion.

The three men were introduced in turn to Leonard Selby, who shook their hands and after a few brief exchanges, which took no more than five minutes, the three strangers departed, with the distinguished bearded man and Sebastian Standish bringing up the rear.

The whole, extremely odd episode was over in less than ten minutes and Selby, still looking relaxed and completely unperturbed, returned to his couch and resumed his television viewing.

Somewhat perplexed, I waited for some further minutes to allow all his visitors' ample time to clear the area and, intrigued and still somewhat confused by what I had just witnessed, stole out of the viewing room to return to my flat, to muse upon this inexplicable and thought provoking incident.

Next morning, whilst walking down the corridor to my office Sebastian Standish, whilst exiting from a nearby lift, called out that he was on his way to a meeting with a Professor Wright and Colonel Thorpe and, if convenient, he would like me join them, adding that he had left a message to that effect on my answer' phone only ten minutes previously.

I was instantly extremely alarmed, near to the point of panic, that my presence in the viewing chamber had been noticed and reported by one of the Colonel's security men who may then have informed Standish or Thorpe but when I entered the room their relaxed demeanour completely reassured me they were completely unaware that I had witnessed the bizarre situation involving the three mystery men.

My relief was reinforced when Colonel Thorpe said they were anxious to share with me some important and exciting information in case Leonard Selby mentioned that he had received some visitors last night and they wished to keep me in the loop.

Feeling rather smug at my clandestine knowledge I was treated by the trio, speaking alternately, expanding upon the strange scenario that I had witnessed the previous evening.

After being formally introduced, Professor Wright explained that no amount of laboratory testing could prove beyond doubt that the spines being discharged from Leonard Selby's palm were still capable of infecting others through normal person to person contact.

Consequently, he had been asked by Colonel Thorpe to provide three "guinea pigs", all chosen for their very long prison terms and who were willing to take part in an experiment to determine, once and for all, whether Leonard Selby's infection remained virulent.

Standish interrupted by expounding that each chosen man, having more than thirty years of incarceration ahead of him, had required little persuasion to take part in, what had been explained to them to be no more than a "safe medical experiment" to assist in the testing of a new influenza drug.

All three men, Thorpe interjected, had also been chosen for their current reasonable good health, no close relatives and relatively low intelligence.

In exchange for their signed and witnessed official acceptance, stating that they had voluntarily agreed to take part in this drug trial, each would be rewarded by an early release, together with a new identity, a significant monetary award and, should they wish, an air ticket to a country of his choice.

On his part, Leonard Selby was merely told that three visiting scientists from another complex, who were currently testing antidotes for obscure infections similar to Leonard Selby's, wished to meet him face to face in order to personally view his condition in order to allow them to better understand his condition.

Standish explained that they required this final piece of the jigsaw to complete a persuasive and more definitive report, to the Home Office, MI5 and the CIA, proving that Leonard Selby was still lethal through mere physical contact.

I was shocked, disgusted and repelled at the callousness and inhumanity of this "so-called experiment" but knew that I had to try hard to hide my true feelings.

Thorpe did not need to add that, should any of the three chosen prisoners survive this "experiment" then their whole diabolical scheme would be in jeopardy and the entire project would, most likely, have to be shelved ...

I prayed, as I have never prayed before, that just one or preferably all these poor deluded victims would somehow survive, not only for their sake but so that I could obtain release from my own enforced incarceration.

I relished the thought that, in the event of their survival, all hopes of rewards, promotion and honours expected by the ruthless and ambitious Colonel and his gang would come to nought.

I still could not believe that my country could ever become involved in such inhuman acts, initially to the three duped prisoners, and eventually to the potential victims, however vile, of this barbarous and malevolent scheme.

The moral depravity of the situation was further emphasised when, some four weeks later, a jubilant Sebastian Standish and the Colonel bumped into me in the corridor and told me that one of the unhappy prisoners had died that night and an autopsy was currently being performed by Thorpe's tame pathologist,

Dr. Grainger to see if the cause of death could be established?

Over the next ten weeks I was telephoned at intervals by an exuberant Colonel Thorpe to inform me that the second and later the third prisoner had died and, far more importantly, all three of the autopsies, undertaken so professionally and skilfully by Dr. Grainger and his team, had failed to pinpoint the nature or category of the poisons that had caused their death ...

... but, a smirking Thorpe had added triumphantly ... "we all know the source of the infection don't we"?

The report by Dr. Grainger, for official records, press and general distribution, concluded that the all victims had died, each due to an invasion of the whole body by a rare pathogenic bacteria, certainly exacerbated by their known previously lifelong drug habits, incarceration and poor general health.

The general public were given the assurance that the infection was extremely rare, not at all contagious to persons of normal health, and with the added assurance that the public should not be, in any way, concerned.

At our next face to face meeting Standish and Thorpe made certain comments that left me in little doubt that, to my great relief, my usefulness to their scheme had diminished.

My relief was mitigated by my sudden realisation that they might be-gin to regard me as a potential problem and a threat to their aims.

Faced with their dilemma that I might expose their scheming, I was certain they would shortly be asking themselves the question ... was I now dispensable and moreover a threat that, however remote, could be tolerated?

Over the next few days my mind was in a complete turmoil over what action I could take to rid myself of this intolerable burden on my conscience and at the same time ensure my own survival now that I had finally tak-en the decision to expose these deranged and dangerous men to the world?

My concern was further increased when, later that week I was present at a talk given by an American scientist, Dr. Frank S. Kelsoe, who had re-cently arrived from the United States with his specialist team.

As he continued speaking it became patently obvious, if there was any doubt remaining in my mind, that the United Kingdom were not acting alone in this gruesome endeavour. His opening comments reinforced that he was operating within a section of the CIA, specialising in the field of highly sophisticated mind-bending techniques.

His presentation included graphically detailed examples showing that some severe mental disorders could be successfully treated by the slow drip feeding of specially formulated chemicals directly into damaged brain cells.

I became increasingly aware that my fellow conspirators were now convinced that Dr. Kelsoe, using these procedures and obviously acting with the full authority of the United States Government, could assist them in manipulating Leonard Selby's thought processes.

He explained that he was convinced that using these same, if slightly modified, techniques, Selby's basic reasoning powers could be gradually enfeebled to more readily accept the aims and objectives of Colonel Thor-pe and his co-conspirators. All Selby's significant medical records had, apparently, been made available to Dr. Kelsoe some months previously and it had had suddenly dawned upon him that, not only he had been granted this absolutely unique opportunity to prove his mad-cap theories, but if successful, would certainly bring him national recognition and si-multaneously guarantee him a place in medical history.

He related, during his detailed treatise, that it was very likely that Selby's brain cells would be even more receptive, than any of his previous patients, due to the fact that his brain cells surely must already have been weakened and made more receptive due to the variety of poisons he had consumed and which were still circulating around his body.

At this point Colonel Thorpe interjected by expressing his belief that the circumstances surrounding the deaths of his son and dearly loved wife would surely be a motivation why he would be a more likely to be more amenable to accept his chosen role as the conspirator's "Saviour of the Free World".

At the conclusion of his talk Thorpe led Dr. Kelsoe from the room with his arm round his shoulder and talking animatedly ... leaving me isolated and in more turmoil.

I had become increasingly sickened at the pitilessness and ruthlessness of those with whom I had unwittingly become entangled. I was left with only one route to follow ... Become a "whistle blower".

I was fully aware that any plan that was not meticulously deployed would be tantamount to signing my own death warrant. The Colonel, now in sight of his goal, would stop at nothing to achieve his objective even, I was convinced, to the extent of ordering my own death should he harbour, even the slightest suspicion that I posed any threat whatsoever to his ultimate dream.

My decision was made a great deal easier by the sudden added realisation that, if I was right in my basic diagnosis that he and his co-conspirators were unbalanced and dangerous megalomaniacs then, after using Selby to eliminate their initial objectives of ISIs, Al-Qaeda, Taliban and other affiliates why should the Colonel and his associates refrain from eliminating any political leader who opposed their own dogmatic domestic political views, both in the United Kingdom and the United States of America?

All listening to this recording may understandably think that I have taken leave of my senses by suggesting that Colonel Thorpe and his supporters, on both sides of the "Pond", would seriously contemplate such a lunatic act, contrary to the very foundations of democracy?

My suspicions were confirmed and indeed reinforced by the response I received as we were all on the point of leaving the meeting room when I foolishly posed the question that there would certainly be influential persons, religious leaders and even some occupants of senior positions within both governments, who would vehemently speak out against the proposed deployment of Leonard Selby, no matter how despicable and dangerous the intended victim?

The Colonel's immediate retort, receiving not a vestige of disapproval or dissent from the rest of the room, was that such persons had better take care or they might find themselves victims of the same treatment currently being planned for our targeted terrorists.

At the time this outrageous statement left me dazed and in turmoil but eventually, on reflection, it only served to validate my firm and unremitting resolve to expose the Colonel and his fellow zealots to the outside world at the first available opportunity.

Chapter 7

JUDGEMENT OF SOLOMON

I had dismissed as complete and utter nonsense the Colonel's retort to my admittedly ill-considered suggestion that the deployment of Leonard Selby as his personal assassin could be thwarted at a stroke by the intervention of just one morally decent, honourable and law-abiding person.

Colonel Thorpe's irrational and ill-judged response by stating that Leonard Selby's virus could be directed against any and all objectors who posed any threat whatsoever to his personal crusade appeared, at the time, to be ludicrous and absurd.

It was only when we received a visit from a George Hornby MP, a junior Home Office Minister who, following an in-depth investigation had suggested that his report to the Home Secretary would be unlikely to be positive, that my mind chillingly returned to his warning.

The Colonel had been informed by letter, some days earlier, that a junior Minister had been specially commissioned by the Home Secretary to conduct an urgent and searching review into the whole Leonard Selby situation.

Apparently, she had been pressured into taking this action following some growing concern recently expressed by her opposite number in the American Senate.

Due to his dual legal and scientific background this particular Minister, George Hornby, had been urgently briefed and given specific instructions to visit the Cambridge Complex for the purpose of undertaking an in-depth investigation and analysis of the feasibility of implementing the "Porcupine Man Project", and to then urgently submit his findings in the form of a confidential report directly to the Home Secretary.

We all, particularly Colonel Thorpe and Dr. Kelsoe, believed that it was reasonable to assume that the choice between a sanctioned implementation or cancellation of the whole project could hinge upon the contents of Hornby's report.

It was obvious from the moment he was introduced to us all that George Hornby was a conservative with a small "C" and was far more concerned about the legal and moral implications surrounding the project than its viability.

Hornby was greeted by Thorpe and Standish and shown into a pleasant room specially designated for his use as a study during his short stay. His first day's work was taken up by everyone within the "inner circle" being separately interviewed and questioned at depth concerning how each person viewed the project.

Just prior to the appointed time of my own interview Colonel Thorpe took me aside and in no uncertain terms warned that I should restrict my responses and comments solely to my medical relationship with Leonard Selby and on no account make reference concerning any other matter connected to the project, ending by reiterating information of which I was already fully aware ... **"George ... you should remember that your every move and comment will be on record"!**

The Colonel, who had already been interviewed, also emphasised that, for the avoidance of doubt, he had informed the Minister that my duties had been strictly confined to the medical wellbeing of Leonard Selby, which had been particularly important following the catastrophic death of Professor Quigley.

Being fully aware of the sophisticated surveillance installed throughout the whole of the Cambridge complex, which would certainly include the particular room chosen by Colonel Thorpe for the Minister, I dismissed my initial reckless thought of surreptitiously passing over some sort of note detailing the full and horrific situation surrounding my patient.

Realising that Thorpe, or one of his cohorts, would certainly be monitoring my every slightest movement and rash comment during my interview with the Minister I reluctantly decided that the risk of disclosure and its unquantifiable consequences was far too great.

In the event, my decision to leave matters to the discretion of this Minister was made infinitely easier by the knowledge, gained from his general tone and demeanour, that George Hornby was his own man and chosen well by the Home Secretary. I was sure that he would have to be thoroughly convinced of each and every aspect of the stratagem being proposed by the Colonel and his entourage before he would submit a report to the Home Secretary that would pave the way for the project to proceed, at least without any imposed restraints.

A penultimate meeting with us all was held following the conclusion of the interviews, which incidentally included a ten-minute "private" session with Leonard Selby.

At our final gathering, prior to the Minister's departure, there were some fraught and occasionally heated exchanges, particularly between the Minister and Colonel Thorpe observed in an embarrassed silence by myself, Sebastian Standish and the American CIA scientist, Dr. Kelsoe.

For my further peace of mind it became increasingly obvious to me, and I am sure to all in that room that, much to the Colonel's increasing exasperation and annoyance, the Minister would, very likely, be advising extreme caution to the Home Secretary with regard to the whole "Porcupine Man" project.

All the Colonel's arguments urging an acceleration of the plan to utilise Leonard Selby to combat the rapidly worsening international situation appeared to fall on deaf ears and in fact, towards the conclusion of the meeting, George Hornby was surprisingly vehement in his criticism of the aims and basic concept of the cabal's enterprise.

Furthermore, he strongly hinted that he viewed the whole project as a scandalous waste of tax payer's money and that its aims may well be viewed as morally demeaning to the two great nations and their allies who were considering participating in this malevolent operation.

The Minister concluded his comments by stating that he felt that it was only fair to warn all in the room that, immediately on his return to his London home, he would be compiling his report which would include his personal opposition to the use of a human being in such an operation, notwithstanding the accepted abhorrence and odiousness of the intended victims.

The Minister added that he felt that the basic concept that he had been presented with was amoral and contrary to all that democracy stood for in a Free World.

Whilst he was also mindful of the aims and advantages hypothe-sised by the Colonel and his followers in deploying Leonard Selby these would have to be carefully balanced against these moral and ethical values.

In response to the Colonel's questioning he reluctantly promised to present a report to the Home Secretary that would contain all the detailed advantages summarised by the Colonel during his interview and it was then up to her, after due consideration, to advise the Prime Minister con-cerning the viability of the project in all its aspects.

My heart leapt when I heard this brave and moral Government Min-ister state, so forthrightly, views that coincided with my own regarding the utilisation of Leonard Selby as an assassin of the State and I could only think about the wholly positive reaction of my erstwhile colleague, Pro-fessor Quigley, had he been alive that day.

As I heard the honest opinions spoken by the Minister my joy was diluted by an inner fear that The Minister had failed to realise that, in Colonel Thorpe, he was dealing a psychopathic mind set and I silently prayed for the Minister to refrain from exposing his innermost thoughts prematurely and restrict these to his private report to the Home Secretary.

Being fully aware that my own position was fragile, and still some-what apprehensive of further inflaming the unhinged Colonel, I felt it appropriate to keep my own council and fervently hope that the Minis-ter's report would be recognised as containing valid arguments against the project and then, presumably following an in-depth discussion involving all participants, appropriately acted upon.

Moreover, I immediately realised, to my added relief, that the Min-ister's report could, at a stroke, remove the necessity for any rash action on my part to expose the Colonel's plans and my relief was palpable.

At our final meeting, just prior to the Minister's departure for Lon-don, we all waited expectantly for the Colonel's response to the Minis-ter's negative tirade and when it finally arrived it was, at least to me, all the more disconcerting for its icy-calm delivery and brevity!

The Colonel quietly replied to the Minister's summing up, his cold eyes boring into Hornby's, in a low voice, completely devoid of any emotion ...

"... So be it Minister!"

Presumably, taking their cue from Colonel Thorpe no one else in the room added one iota of comment to those four simple, but to me ominous words.

Following a very minimal exchange of niceties we all strolled out of the main door to the complex and accompanied the Minister to his private car.

The Minister had previously explained that he had decided to dispense with the services of his official car due to the possible lack of overnight facilities for his chauffeur.

The last we saw of him was his courteous wave as he departed down the long drive to the already open main gates and then presumably via the M11 heading for the capital.

Two days later we were all completely devastated to hear on the Radio and Television channels that a Junior Home Office Minister, George Hornby MP had been found dead by his regular cleaner who had entered the house using her own key.

The tragedy apparently had occurred during the early hours of the morning and it was initially surmised that he had died whilst apparently attempting to tackle a burglar within his London Home.

The report continued that Mr. Hornby's wife and son, who had been enjoying a few days stay at their holiday home near Brighton, had been informed and said to be devastated and in the process of being brought back to London to attend the inquest and initiate the funeral arrangements.

From that day onwards not one word or comment was uttered by the Colonel or any of his entourage concerning the incident involving the Minister's demise and I had neither the courage nor desire to initiate the first move towards any discussion on the matter.

However, in hindsight, I could not dismiss from my mind the request by Frank, the Colonel's right hand man and utterly loyal ex-SAS officer, who had knocked and entered the room during one of our meetings, the day prior to the Minister's departure, and requested the loan of his keys in order that his car could be moved away from a delivery area.

Even at the time I thought that this request was very strange for to my knowledge there was not, and never had been, any delivery area remotely adjacent to where the Minister had parked his car.

Furthermore, I am certain that the Minister handed over his key wallet which must have contained house and other personal keys.

Also it struck me as very odd that Colonel Thorpe firmly instructed Frank, as he was leaving, not to interrupt the meeting again to return the Minister's keys but to leave them in his room on his dressing table.

Within the hour or so before the Minister could reclaim his key wallet copies of any or all of his house keys could easily have been procured.

Surely, It was too much of a coincidence that Frank was absent over the next two days, explained away by the Colonel's vague comment that Frank's mother had been taken seriously ill.

On Franks' return to the complex the following week I obviously enquired about his mother's progress only to be met by a blank stare and some mumbled incoherent comment.

I have no other evidence whatsoever concerning the Colonel's part, if any, in the Minister's murder but it only served to reinforce my own personal resolve to pursue, at the first available opportunity, the brave and ethical stance the Minister took during his visit and which he conveyed so succinctly in an effort to prevent the deployment of Leonard Selby by these misguided and unbalanced zealots.

His honesty and moral fortitude may have signed his own death warrant and during the following days and weeks all the intensive investigations into the perpetrator came to naught.

It appeared that his report to the Home Secretary was never written due to the fact that no document was ever reported to have been found in his home.

The impetus for a new report soon died with the Minister as the intense investigations surrounding the tragedy continued.

The police later reported that the incident was all the more puzzling as their forensic section had reported there appeared to be no forced entry into the Minister's home, no articles were missing and, more importantly, no sign of a struggle.

An old service revolver, discovered near the Minister's body, had been subjected to intensive forensic and ballistic research and was later confirmed as the weapon that had been used to kill the Minister. The police report finally ended by the comment that nothing had been ruled out, including bizarrely, some inference towards possible suicide due to the Minister's fingerprints being found on the weapon.

His wife had declared at the later inquest that she had never seen her husband with any firearm. As far as she was aware he did not possess a firearm licence and had no knowledge of such a weapon in her husband's possession, even though she admitted to the Coroner that her husband had been an active member of the Territorial Army at the time of their marriage.

In the absence of any further evidence the Coroner declared an open verdict.

Some weeks later, following George Hornby's funeral, a smiling Colonel urgently summoned us all to a meeting in his office and, eyes blazing, ecstatically reported that we had been given the final official go-ahead by a communication from the Home Secretary to continue with the deployment of Leonard Selby.

The Colonel explained that her decision was apparently taken on the basis of a package, presumably sealed and ready for delivery by messenger and addressed for the personal and private attention of The Home Secretary which had been found during further searches in the Minister's study by the police.

It was reported that the package contained a DVD disc, the contents of which intimated that George Hornby was preparing to commence writing his detailed report of his visit to Cambridge but that he felt it was his duty to advise the Home Secretary as soon as possible that his full report would be positive in recommending the continuance of the "Porcupine Man Project" together with its urgent implementation!

When I realised the full import of this information was incredulous as the preliminary advice mentioned on this disc was completely at odds to what the Minister had stated prior to his departure to London.

My incredulity was compounded by the failure of the police to find the copious notes that had been taken by the Minister during his visit to

Cambridge which surely would have formed the basis of his full report to the Home Secretary.

This information coupled with the strange situation regarding the Minister's keys and the unscheduled and unexplained absence of the Colonel's right hand man during those crucial days was enough to convince me of the Colonel's involvement in the Minister's murder and the planting of the package containing the DVD.

Chapter 8

CRY HAVOC AND LET SLIP THE DOGS OF WAR

When we were seated in his office later that evening Sebastian Standish reiterated that my job, within their overall scheme of requirements, whilst restricted was nevertheless vital and unequivocal.

My duties were limited to merely continuing to persuade Selby, as his friend and confidant, that by submitting to such invasive and temporally unpleasant treatment the result would be to mankind's ultimate benefit and, moreover I should stress that Dr. Kelsoe's procedures would also aid his full recovery.

I had already decided that I was prepared to accept my unsavoury role on the basis of pure humanity towards Leonard Selby by assisting in making the more evasive treatment as bearable as possible and at concurrently provide me more time to plan my escape.

I had to assume that my every action was under twenty-four hour surveillance by the myriads of cameras dotted around the Cambridge complex and every telephone conversation, both in and out of my flat, was continuously monitored.

"The Porcupine Man", so flippantly named many months ago by Professor Quigley was apparently no longer to be a figment of any one's imagination.

Slowly and surely, through a succession of ruthless, but ingenious medical procedures spread over many weeks and months, Selby was actually persuaded that his "unique gift" presented him the opportunity to avenge the death of his wife and son and simultaneously serve his country.

In addition to the experimental mind-bending techniques and the concurrent chemical infusions directly into Selby's brain, the poor man was also subjected to a programme of sleep deprivation, hypnosis and autosuggestion.

As the weeks became months Selby's resistance gradually succumbed to these pressures and he eventually began to accept the controlling influences of his tormentors.

My own involvement in all these procedures was thankfully gradually reduced to a point when I became just a mere observer.

Computer-aided flashbacks presented Leonard Selby with the simulated last seconds of his son's death, combined with the photo-images of other young, vulnerable, defenceless victims of the activities of these terrorists.

During what was to be my last brief and somewhat distressing meeting with Leonard Selby he appeared to be in a zombie-like state, his conversation somewhat stilted and restricted to endlessly repeating, in a monotone voice, that it was his moral duty to use "his gift" to avenge his wife, his son and his country.

A delusional Leonard Selby had finally been persuaded that, by his participation in his violent and murderous assignments, he would eventually gain mental tranquillity and peace of mind which would eventually enable him to return to live a normal life.

Some days later, whilst still musing over my own situation and vainly trying to plan my next move, the strident door bell of my flat brought me back to reality, the open door revealed a visibly exultant and triumphant Standish.

Once inside my sitting room he relished imparting the news that Selby's transformation, from suburban Chemist to silent assassin, had been finally achieved far beyond even his and Colonel Thorpe's wildest expectations.

He even intimated that Selby had already performed even further several successful contact "killings" on command ... whether human or animal I was never informed and indeed I had no compulsion or desire to enquire further.

Even though I was convinced that Standish was still completely unaware of the clandestine knowledge resulting from what I had witnessed from the dark viewing gallery, the revulsion in my eyes coupled with my silence at his news must have finally marked me down as an untrustworthy liability.

Standish, surprisingly even let slip that experiments, touched upon by the American Frank Shelton some months previously, were even being currently undertaken in America that would eventually remove the ne-

cessity for Leonard Selby to be in direct contact with any intending victim by harvesting these independently active deadly spines continuously being emitted from Selby's palm wound. These would then be placed within some item that would eventually be reasonably expected to be handled by any targeted victim.

His closing remarks made it perfectly obvious that I no longer had any role to play concerning Leonard Selby thus confirming that, alarmingly, I was now possibly being regarded as dispensable element within this close knit group of fanatics.

My instincts were proved correct as the next day I found that my pass no longer allowed me access, even to my own laboratory. The guards, politely but firmly, advised me to contact Mr. Standish for any further explanations.

On telephoning Standish's office, to register my objections to my shabby treatment, his private secretary, Anne, informed me that she had already sent an urgent email to my office computer demanding my presence at a meeting that afternoon which, to my astonishment, was actually scheduled to take place in Leonard Selby's own private apartment.

I arrived at the hospital entrance at the appointed time and I immediately sensed some dramatic change in the atmosphere surrounding the whole area.

To add to my utter confusion and astonishment there was a complete absence of guards in the corridor or security desks and in somewhat of a daze I entered Selby's apartment through a fully open and completely unguarded door.

I was faced with a stripped bed and the heavy curtains fully drawn back, bathing the empty room in the early morning sun.

Hearing someone else entering the room I turned and recognised Sebastian Standish's taciturn Personal Assistant, a Michael Gray, who silently handed over a buff coloured envelope with the words:

"Private and strictly confidential" highlighted in red above my name.

The hand-written letter contained information that was short, terse and to the point and from the whole tone of the letter I did not even need to glance at the signature ... Sebastian Standish ... it coldly explained that he very much regretted to inform me that Leonard Selby had unfortunately finally succumbed to his infection and had died peacefully that night in his sleep.

Standish thanked me for my services, concluding his letter with a highlighted reminder of my duty to maintain complete and absolute secrecy concerning my involvement with Leonard Selby under the Secrecy Act I had signed at the commencement of my engagement in the Colonnade Hotel.

A generous cheque was enclosed in full and final settlement of all matters connected to my contract to which was attached a glowing letter of recommendation for any prospective new employer.

I stood transfixed in the middle of the room and I must admit to being completely and utterly stunned at this unforeseen turn of events, particularly as during my visit the previous day, I had found Leonard in reasonably good physical health considering the ordeal he had been subjected to over the past months.

The next day, feeling that a huge load had been removed from my shoulders, I ate my first hearty breakfast in many months.

Even though obviously saddened by this bombshell my feelings were ameliorated by my intense and overwhelming relief that Leonard Selby had finally found peace but, far more importantly, the realisation slowly dawned on me that the whole ghastly episode, not least the burning question of whether or not to disclose the Leonard Selby situation to the world, had finally been resolved by his death.

There was now no need to place my life at risk by disclosing what had occurred at Cambridge and I could finally proceed with my life and career with an easy conscience.

My breakfast completed, I flopped down in my easy chair with a mug of tea, completely overwhelmed by a feeling of intense relief and peace of mind that is hard to describe, but eternally thankful that all of the combined evil and warped ambitions of Thorpe, Standish and Dr. Kelsoe had been finally thwarted by a simple act of nature.

Chapter 9

ILLUMINATING THE DARKNESS

The constant and intense mental strain of the past months had taken its toll on my health and, feeling worn out mentally and physically exhausted, I made the decision to arrange a well-earned holiday in the South East of England resort of Southwold, perhaps enjoying the luxury of the Swan Hotel and spoiling myself with the famous local oysters and sampling the area's real ale.

After nearly two weeks on the coast, and approaching my old self, I grew increasingly bored with this life of leisure and inactivity and, aided by Standish's excellent reference, I very soon obtained a position with a world renowned pharmaceutical company.

I looked forward to initially commencing work at their Head Office in London in five weeks time, with a promise that in due course I would be directing a team of scientists, operating from their South American subsidiary, to commence investigations into obscure tropical diseases deep within the Brazilian jungles.

After a great deal of soul-searching I decided that I needed to divorce myself completely from my past life and start afresh and consequently I resolved to dispose of my old log cabin in the High Peak District.

Having spent most of the previous week meeting Chartered Surveyors from the local estate agents I received a telephone call from one of the Partners of a local property company assuring me that, due to the current high demand for luxury log cabins in the area, a sale would seem to be no problem and to my delight an offer was soon made which I accepted.

It was arranged that they would complete if I could wait until they had finalised the sale of their own property which I readily agreed, due to their obvious love of the area, underwritten by the comfort of a significant deposit.

Their offer included all the cabin's minimal furnishings which thankfully removed the need to visit the cabin again to arrange their disposal in the months before the new owners could finalise their purchase of my cabin.

Resuming my hectic London life the months passed quickly and I was thoroughly enjoying my financial independence together with the stimulating challenge of my new position and looking forward to my imminent transfer to South America when my tranquillity was shattered by the headlines in my morning paper.

The heavy black type hit me between the eyes! ...

... An extreme and notorious Middle Eastern Leader and two of his lieutenants, all avid supporters of ISIS had all died within a six-week period, after finally succumbing to a mystery infection that had baffled doctors ...

The lurid details within the article, even though phrased in sensational journalistic jargon and unsupported by any detailed scientific or medically instructive information, naturally awakened my professional interest and I spent the remainder of the day on my computer seeking further information, without any substantive success.

Even with this very limited information, emanating from a junior reporter more interested in the drama of the situation rather than providing any medical or scientific details, the combination of the articles and the subsequent television reports all combined to send a chilling blast to my brain that I found hard to dismiss.

At waking intervals during a restless night I dissected the mass of information that I had gleaned both from the internet and the many conflicting press details, over and over again in my mind.

The television channels the following day concentrated on the more lurid and sensational aspects of the illnesses of the three men, describing their sufferings over periods which, despite all receiving intensive treatment, had varied from a few weeks to some months before eventually all three had fallen into a deepening coma and finally death had ensued.

No matter how hard I tried I found it impossible to dismiss my increasing belief that I had witnessed this whole scenario ... with the exception of the actual death of my patient ... many months before in Cambridge.

One of the dead men was highlighted within the more lurid sections of the press, as being a man despised and feared as a leading instigator of terrorism in his region and, yet another headline article written by the diplomatic correspondent of The Times newspaper, mentioned that some Western Governments had expressed their somewhat hypocritical diplomatic condolences.

Completely lacking any further substantive information I was on the point of dismissing the news from my mind when a short paragraph, hidden within another newspaper article, hit me like a thunderbolt!...

"... our research has revealed that a low-key deputation from the United Kingdom had met with the now deceased despot and his entourage some three months earlier in a sensitive and clandestine effort to negotiate the repatriation of some hostages held by their terrorist organisation."

... and directly underneath the article was a small grainy, photograph of this deputation highlighting, by superimposed white rings the three, now deceased, men.

But my attention was immediately drawn to the sight of what appeared to be a very familiar face of a tall man standing at the rear of the group and, with a trembling hand I reached for my magnifying glass and trained it on the image ... the person on the back row was unmistakably that of Colonel Thorpe and to his immediate left was another familiar face ... but how could that possibly be so?

... This second man in the photograph was dead ... the Coroner had given his carefully considered verdict based upon the detailed statements of nurses and other hospital staff, confirmed by the indisputable verbal and written medical evidence presented to him for his consideration in arriving at his final judicious decision.

Moreover, I had attended his funeral in a Cambridge church, and even been persuaded by Colonel Thorpe and Dr. Kelsoe to present his eulogy.

I had even witnessed, with my own eyes, his brass handled oak coffin being lowered slowly into an open grave.

Even though heavy glasses now framed his pale face, further magnifica-
tion of the grainy image allowed no doubt in my mind that this was the
face of my old patient, Leonard Selby! … back from the dead?

A multitude of questions bounced around within my brain and each respond-
ing answer to each question was too horrific for me to immediately grasp.

If Leonard Selby was still alive why had I been duped, along with the
whole country, not least the medical and legal profession, into believing
that Selby had died in the Cambridge complex, many months previously?

I read and re-read the pages of the paper finally returning to check
and re-check the photograph with my mind a tumbling turmoil of an-
swers and questions! … questions and answers! … all hammering at my
brain in quick succession.

Regularly pouring over newspaper reports during the succeeding months I
noticed further press and television reports mentioning that other terrorist
leaders, having either been struck down, or dying from sudden mysterious
illness and it was the subject of conjecture, by some commentators, that
these latter terrorists may have been in personal contact with the original
victims and caught some obscure infection.

One minor item that I noticed in one of the tabloid papers was that,
it had been rumoured that Britain had recently commenced paying clan-
destine ransoms to certain terrorist factions, in direct contravention of their
long established policy.

The United Kingdom, in line with the United States had always main-
tained that paying cash ransoms to obtain the release of their nationals
encouraged further kidnapping and bolstered the recipient's ability to pur-
chase more arms and sophisticated armoured vehicles.

Both governments had previously constantly refused to pay or even
discuss the handing over of any ransom and had even criticised any Eu-
ropean country that had been involved in such practises.

Evidence of some returning, previously held American nationals, re-
inforced my suspicion that the reports concerning this change in policy
by the United Kingdom could be true … I wondered why this dramatic
change in policy had been sanctioned until some headlines reported that

several important leaders of the same organisations that had returned their captors, following the receipt of a ransom, had died some months later.

My thoughts immediately returned to the comment made by Sebastian Standish and American Frank Shelton, so many months ago, that it was even feasible for these deadly infected spines could be harvested from Selby and some ingenious way could be found for the chosen recipient to be infected.

Surely the ransom money, paid over to the terrorists had not been seeded with Selby's deadly spines?

This, if true, could explain everything ... not least the dramatic change of mind, by both the United Kingdom and the United States, never to pay ransoms under any circumstances.

Each reported incident reinforced my belief, however unreal, firstly that Leonard Selby had not died in that Cambridge complex and secondly, that the unholy trinity of Thorpe, Standish and Dr. Kelsoe had succeeded in perfecting their angel of death.

It was after reading a further report of the demise of yet another notorious terrorist leader that I made, in an impulsive moment of complete and utter madness, the most stupid decision of my whole life.

Even now, after calm reflection, I can only explain my action as the result of my common sense being usurped by a cocktail of fear and stress as I fatally tapped the keys on my mobile to connect me to Colonel Thorpe.

The moment I heard his answering voice I knew that I would live to regret my impulsive action but, for my own sanity, I required to know the all the answers to the questions that were incessantly hammering inside my head.

The Colonel's overtly friendly response to my call should have been the only warning I needed to cut short the conversation or rapidly invent some vapid, innocuous reason for calling him and then hope that he would forget I ever existed.

Throughout my long association with the Colonel he had never, for one instant, been friendly ... Courteous, Yes! Polite, Yes! but friendly was alien and contrary to his whole nature.

I hesitatingly posed my question to the Colonel that really did not require any confirmation ... Is Leonard Selby still alive?

I did not even hear his reply and, to this day, I cannot recollect the whole of our conversation apart from his absolute insistence on knowing from where I was speaking and demanding an immediate face to face meeting at which he promised he would satisfy all my questions.

I assure my listeners to this recording that I have no intention of meeting with the Colonel or any of his entourage or even contacting them in the future.

It is my sincere hope that, when you are listening to this message, I will be far away from England, likely never able to return.

I again apologise to all my listeners for the length and detail comprising this recorded warning but perhaps the detail offered will enable each and every recipient of my message to check and recheck the historical events leading up to the present day and act.

It is my belief that these evil and misguided people need to face justice and their actions neutralised without any further delay.

Sincerely,
George Manjon Deakin.

Chapter 10

ALL IS LOST SAVE HONOUR

George sighed with a mixture of relief, weariness and resignation as he completed his task by finally taking the ten separately copied recordings over to his desk and carefully placing them within the top drawer of his bureaux, looking forward to a good night's sleep to prepare him for the day ahead.

Refreshed, he awoke early and, after showering and shaving he wandered, dressed only his thick cotton robe, into his kitchen to prepare a breakfast of eggs, toast and marmalade, finally washed down with copious quantities of dark coffee.

Dressed in the same clothes as the previous day, George then wandered into the sitting room and opened the bureaux drawer to remove the recordings and placed each in separate thick manila envelope which he carefully addressed to their respective recipients.

He intended to send these by first class recorded delivery via the local village post office, which he would pass on his way to the M1 and Heathrow Airport.

When the envelopes had been double sealed with plastic tape and placed within his brief case, he finally snapped the brass lock shut and placed the case on the easy chair in the corner of the room.

Purely as an afterthought, seeing that he had left the master disc on the top of his desk George hesitated, looked around and finally placed the disc within an old plastic Tesco bag, tied the handles and placed it inside an old cardboard box.

The envelope he placed inside contained a request that if the box was ever found the contents should immediately be taken by hand, to the address printed in bold type on the side.

Finally, purely as an afterthought, George tucked two fifty pound notes inside to defray any costs the unknown finder might incur.

His last act was to think about a suitable hiding place, but one that might conceivably be stumbled upon at a later date. He finally deciding upon a dusty shelf in the corner of his near empty log-store, situated some fifty yards from his main cabin.

His job completed, George strolled back to his log cabin, entered and, after turning the key in the lock, rammed home the wrought iron bolts to his back door, finally replaced the recording machine back in the pine cupboard snapping the door shut.

Gathering his jacket and the previously packed bags he again checked that his external doors were secured, the mains water had been turned off and a welcome note with a list of where to find the cabin's other services and miscellaneous meters was left on the table to assist the new owners.

Taking a last fond farewell look around his lounge he turned and entered his garage by the inside connecting fire door.

Having stowed his baggage, together with his leather brief case containing the ten addressed envelopes in the boot he wearily slid into the driver's seat and pressed the remote control to open the garage door.

As the slowly ascending door revealed the outside world George Deakin gasped as he viewed three threatening black limousines blocking his exit with the grim faces of Colonel Thorpe and Sebastian Standish seated in the middle car ...

The following extract appeared in the local press some weeks later:

Tragedy in the Peak District of Derbyshire.
We regret having to report the tragic death of the local owner of a log cabin holiday home, situated in remote woodlands between Chesterfield and Matlock in the heart of the Derbyshire High Peak District.
Early reports indicate that George Deakin, a forty-seven year old, well respected research scientist, had succumbed

to the effects of carbon monoxide poisoning whilst seated in his car within his garage, which had been locked and its door internally sealed.

A spokesman for one of his previous employers, a Colonel Thorpe, issued a statement expressing his condolences to the family of the deceased, adding that his erstwhile friend and colleague had, earlier in the year, given notice after a period of extreme clinical depression following the sudden and tragic death of his colleague, the eminent Professor Raymond Quigley.

All his friends and colleagues had hoped that his new appointment, which would have eventually involved working overseas, could have aided his recovery but sadly this appears not to have been the case.

At the inquest, hurriedly convened to investigate the circumstances surrounding Mr. Deakin's death, a previous colleague of the deceased, a Dr. Grainger, confirmed to the Coroner that he had been treating Mr. Deakin for depression for some considerable time.

Following the submissions to the Court, including exhaustive police investigations, the Coroner's verdict was recorded that, upon the evidence that had been placed before him, George Deakin had sadly taken his own life whilst the balance of his mind had been disturbed, most likely as a result of his chronic depression.

EPILOGUE

... A log store at the rear of a remote log cabin was already being overgrown by weeds and creepers when, some months following George Deakin's funeral, the new owners of his cabin, a married professional couple with two young children, excitedly arrived to take possession of their remote country retreat, to enjoy the peace and solitude of the surrounding Peak District.

The approaching winter was the time when the local fuel company would most certainly be contacted with requests to top-up the log stores for all the houses and cabins in the area.

This would include the incoming family's log store complete with its secret, still reposing within its dark depths ...

... a Tesco bag within a box labelled **"TOP SECRET"**.

Children love to explore the garden and out-houses of a new home and one day the more inquisitive child will excitedly bring a small dusty cardboard box back to his parents and perhaps, in spite of all their precautions and their many nefarious actions, the conspirators will eventually be brought to justice and the truth finally exposed to a shocked and unbelieving world? ...

... the real truth concerning the Porcupine Man!

EIN HERZ FÜR AUTOREN A HEART FOR AUTHORS À L'ÉCOUTE DES AUTEURS MIA KAPΔIA ΓIA ΣY
HJÄRTA FÖR FÖRFATTARE UN CORAZÓN POR LOS AUTORES YAZARLARIMIZA GÖNÜL VERELIM
CUORE PER AUTORI ET HJERTE FOR FORFATTERE EEN HART VOOR SCHRIJVERS TEMOS OS AU
HERZÖINKÉRT SERCE DLA AUTORÓW EIN HERZ FÜR AUTOREN A HEART FOR AUTHORS À L'ÉC
RAÇÃO ВСЕЙ ДУШОЙ К АВТОРАМ ETT HJÄRTA FÖR FÖRFATTARE Á LA ESCUCHA DE LOS AU
UTEURS MIA KAPΔIA ΓIA ΣYΓΓPAΦEIΣ UN CUORE PER AUTORI ET HJERTE FOR FORFATTERE EE
ARLARIMIZA GÖ RE ZÖINKÉRT SERCE DLA AUTORÓW EIN HERZ F
OR SCHRIJVERS OS OF RAÇÃO ВСЕЙ ДУШОЙ К АВТОРАМ ETT HJÄRTA I

The author

Peter M. Sellers was born in 1932. He was edu-
cated at The Hulme Grammar School, Oldham,
Lancashire. His favourite activities are antiques and
woodland management. He is a Chartered Survey-
or with forty-six years' experience within a major
Civil Engineering PLC company, followed by five
years as Scottish and Northern England Consultant
to the Denham Syndicate at Lloyd's Underwriters.
He was engaged as visiting lecturer by Manches-
ter University for five years on Civil Engineering
law and contract procedure. He operated his own
company for fifteen years, advising and acting for
construction companies involved in claims and
disputes.
He is married to Margaret and has two children.
His only other two literary efforts were in self-pub-
lishing, including the first ever book written
recording the history and manufacture of glass
ornaments made from dumped glass entitled,
"Victorian Dumps, Paper Weights, Mantel Ornaments, Doorstops & Whimsies 1820–1914" which
was followed by "The Anatomy of a Construction
Company, 1934–2006".